Potomac Review

Published by the Paul Peck Humanities Institute at
Montgomery College, Rockville
51 Mannakee Street, Rockville, MD 20850

Potomac Review has been made possible through
the generosity of Montgomery College.

A special thanks to Dean Rodney Redmond.

For submission guidelines and more information:
http://www.potomacreview.org

Potomac Review, Inc. is a not-for-profit 501 c(3) corp.
Member, Council of Literary Magazines & Presses
Indexed by the American Humanities Index
ISBN: 978-0-9889493-5-5
ISSN:10073 – 1989

SUBSCRIBE TO *POTOMAC REVIEW*

One year at $24 (2 issues)
Two years at $36 (4 issues)
Sample copy order, $10 (Single issue)

Cover photo by Ryan McGuirea
Cover and interior design by Carol Chu

TABLE OF CONTENTS

FICTION

NONFICTION

SIT STILL

Kyle Hays

This part of life should get to be longer. This day, on your eighth birthday, getting to go to your first professional baseball game with your father, is already streaking by with a tangent of minutes. Your father is letting you skip summer school today. As he starts the car, your father mentions something about both of you taking a little hiatus from home. This is your happiest experience so far in such a young life.

Maybe those past seven years, ones you can remember, were good to you—though there's no real objective image of what a "good" first seven years should be like, but you were more or less happy, so to speak. But this last year, your eighth year, piled miracles on you: (1) Fear incited by your Babe Ruth lamp's fluorescent quivers, propped next to the bed, lessened. (2) Something your mother called, in soft mutterings not meant for you to hear, her "diagnosis." (3) Living or having lived next to a busy residential intersection, an ambulance carried away—on a crowded street—a man who had crashed into a telephone pole, hanging waist out from his car. Taking care of oneself is a value, or so said your father. (4) Those drives to the hospital—with you in the front seat, next to your father, catching glimpses of your mother's head against the rear window through the immaterial and hazy distance of the passenger side mirror—were spiritual exercises in physical form and movement. (5) After the funeral, your father asked if you were going to be okay, and you asked him if *he* was going to be okay. You both said "yes," but still you didn't understand honesty, because, like your father, you told no-one anything, separating yourself from experiences.

And words. New and difficult words creeped into your lexicon, your never really knowing how they were used in everyday speech: *Malignant. Chemotherapy. Immediate Extension of Outflow Datum. Gamma Wave Inactivity.* Some words can kill you with their consistent echo, lodging themselves into your underdeveloped heart to pleat infinitely.

The stadium is, when it comes into view after the car divides away from traffic towards the green stadium exit sign, a static object against a system of movement. Cars twist and meander between municipal-orange traffic cones. Your father is several steps ahead, ignoring unauthorized street vendors in the parking lot who are trying to sell him overpriced bottles of water, lugging their ice chests behind them. ROW Q-6. Your ballcap is too tight around your head. Birds pick up and discard dropped cigarettes and stale food. Shuttle buses pass and you wave at those who paid a little more for comfort. Look above. Clouds lose their color to match the sky, casting rolling shadows over the various and calculated foliage that leads away from the parking lot. Even the sun shifts the landscape behind waves that are only exclusive in this kind of summer heat. But only the stadium, as you move closer, swells to encompass the horizon. A kind of preoccupied singularity in a space surrounded by steel and pavement. The stadium's shadow glides to your waist. Gravity seems to get heavier with every step, and it outweighs the knowledge of knowing where you are. Every crack in the soft-red brick of the stadium is so much clearer than what you've seen on television. Everything is still moving.

For me, walking into the player's entrance masks all aspects of metropolitan nearness. Walking through the tunnel to the locker room, most players are slightly aware how each previous game fades so rapidly from memory, all of it so vivid each night we play but fades with each established rhythm of professional routine—every overhead lamp's bright and tense light concentrates the confines of remembrance. There are a dozen photographers and journalists in the press room waiting for some comments on the trade deadline. Each one barks questions as the coach steps out of his office. We don't make eye contact when he passes. Such tremendous pressure is on the front office to make some moves. You'll never see this aspect of the game.

Outside the stadium, you can only see the brightness the game has to offer. Everything around the stadium is enormously lighthearted as only a carnival or fair could do: eighteen-inch corndogs sold with lemonade, over-priced stuffed toys, every leg khakied, every waist fanny-packed, a child riding on a parent's shoulders. Your father rubs sunscreen on your face, the cold and oily cream a relief from the blistering and rosy-skinned heat. He places a heavy dollop of the cream under his nose and twists his face to make you laugh. He's trying to read your reaction. Living in that instant, you feel yourself above all others.

Now, from the twenty-five-dollar-a-spot parking lot with faded, white lines and glimmering cars, you're waiting within the serpentine line of ticket holders. There are others around your age—some older, some younger—standing in this same line, all surrounded by adult discourse and argument, a kinetic impulse of the spectators' spirit. And you grip your father's hand as you volley complaints about the achingly slow march into the stadium, all the while being restless, displaying almost infantile outbursts, never understanding there's a presiding metaphor for a dutiful and respected economy.

"Stand still," he says, your father.

And it's the waiting that gives everything a flat regularity—where all time and all motion funnels towards the gates. The ticket-taker, not caring, who doesn't pay any attention to all those passing him by, takes your ticket—which your father let you hold—with a slender and impeccable personal smoothness and rips it. As you move through the entranceway, the rhythms of the stadium grounds catch you on the entry: the clank and click of ticket gates, revolving. Other people nudge and brush past—the forking V towards either direction with every person moving with a well-mannered precision. Trash cans already overflowing. An elderly lady, with an overly cautious effort, tries to dip her pretzel in liquid yellow cheese and still drops all of it on the ground. Employees in neon yellow shirts with "Staff" block-lettered on the back hand out promotional bobbleheads for the first fifteen-thousand lucky fans, which you were one. And although you wanted the bobblehead of David Gonzalez—your favorite player—you got me instead. Everything seemingly predetermined. Like a stage. Like a clock. Behind *It's A Hot Dawg!* there's the insectile hiss of toilets flushing with an industrial-grade strength. As you wait for your father to pass through the gates, you notice almost every head is ball-capped and every face streaked white with sunscreen, including your father's.

Since changing schools, friends have been hard to come by. At your age, friends are determined more by proximity than actual choosing. The newly built apartment building's tenants are professional looking and always nod to you in the hallways as they pass with a bustling and lonely resilience to wherever they sell their specialized services. Though there's a playground next to the pool, no kids—from what you've gathered—have ever played on it. But still there did spring something resembling hope when your father asked if you wanted to have a party with some of the local kids, but it's in the way he asked, a kind of irrelevance, a rigidity that hoped not to intrude, that made you say "No." Somehow you knew he couldn't handle a party without seeing your mother bring out the cake. Did it start then? Did it start at that moment or was it earlier when he sectioned off his room in your original house and he slept on the floor? Did it start when he wore sunglasses at the funeral? What was the moment you understood your father's limits for the first time? All children reach that point sometime in their lives. And there, as you stared at him, was a collision of emotions and thoughts that wore across his face: a nature of the recent history involved with the embarrassing irrevocability of parental love. "Okay," he said. It's impossible to look at what we love without failure.

And that is why, with your father's hand on your back, guiding you towards your seats, it is so important for you to show your father you are grateful. Wear a smile like how hot winds smother summer afternoons. Look up. Make sure he sees you smiling. You accidentally run into the ass of an elderly lady, though not the same lady who dropped the pretzel. Apologize. You are polite, or so says your father—you like the way he takes pride in your politeness. The tunnel leading you to your seats is crowded and dark, and you don't think he's seen you smile yet, but when you finally reach the end of the tunnel, the air seems to open with an unmatched clarity you didn't know could exist. Birds scissor past. A lone paper airplane, thrown from the stands above, dives below and out of view. The buttery whiff of popcorn. Wind threatens to push you back into the tunnel. Listen. Only half-filled, the stadium still produces a never-ending roar as if it's waiting to come back in on itself. Scan across. The whole inner bowl of the stadium is in a constant, unnerving pulse—of people looking for their seats—like a deep and difficult swallow. All this movement excludes order. And the degree to which you are involved keeps you apart from the pageantry of being in a crowd. Look down. The concentric and obtusely angled rows and sections of stadium seating stretch to a narrow point where muraled, Krylon numbers give notice to where you are, where you're supposed to be. By the left-field wall, stadium maintenance inserts new bulbs for the sterile red lights of the pitch count. A carpet of green grass expands towards dead center and the ragged, steel edge of the city around you. All this, here, in the southwest corner of Dallas.

People turn their heads as you shout "Whoa" and "Wow" with a genuine excitement. It surprises you how there's a real assurance of sanctity in sincerity. And now you're caught between the fissure of authentic and insincere facial expressions.

You over correct. It's impossible for someone to actually be this excited. Tone it down. Just carry on this gentle smile until your face begins to hurt.

Take each step down the steep staircase carefully. Concentrate. The sun burns through the roars around you. Hold on tight to the railing. The metal railing is hot as you slide your hand down it. You pass other people already in their seats. Some are taking pictures of the stadium. More are applying too much sunscreen to their children or taking sips from their over-sized souvenir cups. A young girl is resting her head against her mother's shoulder, already bored.

Your seat is on the first row of the balcony over the VISITOR's dugout. As of right now, no one else is in your row, except your father. Push the foldable seat down. Feel the warmth of stadium seating plastic beneath you. The cement below your feet is grey like these last few clouds over the city. Your father sits next to you and comments on the view. Keep smiling. Tell him "Thank you." He looks over and gives you a nod that he recognizes your appreciation, but you still notice the distance in his face that's been present for most of this past year. Climb up to the protective railing. Look over. The whole platform overhangs the seats below, and everything, from this angle, feels still and quiet. Wind thickens around your head—time, too. Above the balcony's slanting shadow, time doesn't pass at all. Every heartbeat is felt in your head as blood rushes towards it. The ballcap's pressure amplifies this feeling. Below. Rows of people produce a mass of activity and motion that constricts your chest. If you wanted, you could watch what happens below you forever.

"Sit back," says your father.

You ask again what time the game will start, and your father points to the corner of the scoreboard. Some of those section's bulbs are out, making it look like the starting time is at 04:UU. Your father asks if you want a soda, and you say "Yes, sir." As he leaves for the concession stand, you watch the few players still warming up on the field. Playing catch. Running along the divide of outfield grass and the red dirt of the warning track. Seeing the players on the field seems limited at this distance. Perception, from here, diminishes the balletic and frenetic motion of what happens on the field. Every ball thrown or hit loses its bend through time and space, and you get to watch only the speed of the ball as if everything else is encased in glass and the ball is the only thing illuminated.

There's some bickering about the blue alternate home jerseys we're wearing today. We haven't won a game in them all season. Down below the stands, under the home dugout, there's the spicy scent of cheap body deodorant and mentholated, pain-relieving rubs. Coach stands there, taking in each complaint, too preoccupied with other cares, waiting for us to end our gripes, and mumbles some words about not confusing black miracles with mental mistakes. Each of us believes the whole game boils down to sacrifice and superstitions. Like a Greek temple. Like a Catholic mass. But then, even deeper down—where we all know but don't ever say it out loud—we're wrong; we're all just stunningly mediocre. The analysts say so. Our nine-game losing streak is definitely some sort of commentary. But we still put on our jerseys, which always have a surprising polyester weight to them—much different from the three-button athletic shirts your peewee team wears with "Rico's Taco Palace's Hot Tamales" screen-printed on the front—and head towards the player's tunnel.

The national anthem is a slight but traditional pause within the starting mechanism of the game, a kind of starting gun allowing the crowd's reaction to focus away from individual interactions and coalesce to a point until the whole stadium joins in the same, well-intentioned but poor a cappella. Hum along. Your ballcap is over your heart. Everyone with a ballcap is in the same pose as you. No one explained why this gesture is so important, what it signifies. And after the song finishes and after some local celebrity throws the ceremonial first pitch wildly high, we take the field to start the game.

Jogging to left field always feels lonely to me, even though thirty-thousand people are circled around, watching. The odors of the stadium are lost on this level. For the crowd, the culture of the stadium is in the fragrances. For the player, the odors of the game are vague and fleeting, entirely abstract and disloyal.

Under my cleats, the grass is soft, matted. Under your feet, there are peanut shells from yesterday's crowd that weren't properly swept away. Starting lineups are announced by the garish boom of the announcer's voice. The crowd is always in a frenzy when the game first starts. Some are already faltering in their enthusiasm due to the heat. You don't mind the heat so much. Not here to come and to see, you want to be hooked in the innocent combination of spectacle and gritty enchantment that the game offers, and, as the umpire announces it's time to "play ball," you climb up to the protective railing to watch. The game moves with a speed and precision you can't believe—more uniform and intentional than your peewee leagues. From this distance, the ball blurs from the pitcher's mound to home plate. Up here, you're not even sure the pitcher is throwing anything at all. The only way you know is the confirmatory pop of the catcher's glove.

First pitch of the game is a ball. Your father cups his hands around his mouth and boos, and you imitate him. You try to lean against the railing again, but your hands slightly slip. Your father grabs you, and says something concerning danger. You can tell he is both worried and angry. The only noise you can hear is the background noise of people talking.

You both fall back into your seats, and your father's posture is more or less the same as yours: slightly forward, elbows on the knees, but he is not resting his face in his hands like you currently are. His hands are out in front of him—causing a right angle of sorts—where both hands' thumbs and forefingers are touching, creating a diamond shape space between them. In this position, he switches from staring at the action happening on the field in an aloof, hazy way to looking down at the space between his hands with concern.

Without even having to look up, you can tell the sun's position in the sky just by where it's hottest on your skin. "It's hot," you say. This is a safe thing to say. All through this whole last black year, you've found a few stock phrases that would lead to cautious, low-risk conversations with your father. These were so obviously forced that you felt even more distance between the two of you than before the words took hold in the world, because these conversations didn't ease any kind of burden or erase any kind of grief: they simply reminded you two of what wasn't there any more. Both of you feel as if you're withering in place, atrophy taking hold in the structure of familial complexity and comfort. Your father responds with a John Wayne impression, and you laugh, even though I know you don't know who John Wayne is, and you feel there's a particular response required of you, but you're not sure what.

Everyone watches as Kastl bounces two more in the dirt, and on the next pitch as Dixson, too eager, flies out to center. Washington hits a chopper to third, easy out. Kenn is rung up on three pitches to end the top half of the first on a strikeout. A backwards "K" is shown on the scoreboard—one of the lights struggles to come on, stunting the bottom leg of the letter—and the crowd leaps into noise and joy as the catcher's mitt pops, but they just as quickly fall back into a dense murmur.

Not bringing your glove with you blemishes the day. Every prospect of taking home a foul ball, those rare and sought-after souvenirs, diminishes every time you feel the wind across your ungloved hand. Turning towards your father, you ask him if he'll catch the ball if it comes near you. Though hot dog vendors are everywhere, your father is too busy trying to get the attention of one to hear you. There's some awkward apologizing as your father steps into another person's footpath. You, reluctantly, let the subject go. Television has ruined your sense of the game. You don't believe foul balls could ever reach this high, anyway. One-hundred-nineteen baseballs are used on average per game. This is a statistic you don't know. It's unlikely one will reach up here, you think. Signs are posted every fifteen feet along the rail concerning the dangers of flying objects, but these only obstruct the view. Many foul balls end up amongst the crowd but are rarely shown going into the stands. For most of the time, the gaze of the camera isn't interested in happenings outside the lines of the game.

During the middle of the second inning, the mascots take the field to race around the bases. "Your mother's favorite part of the game were the mascots," says your father. This is also something you didn't know. You get the urge to bring out the photo of your mother you keep within your plastic, velcro wallet, but you notice a beginning arc of a smile on your father's face as the mascots start running the bases, and the rarity of seeing your father smile makes your heart droop like a dying toy. Your father reminds you of something evaporating. Like steam. Like something elusively simmering and vaporous.

Time feels compressed during the first three innings of any game, folds every action and reaction up, and when you think the game will simply blink by, time unfolds and it feels as if these middle innings have taken weeks—every game folding and unfolding like a hospital bed.

Now, in the bottom of the fifth, when David comes up for his second plate appearance—with one double already roped to left-center—there's talk in the dugout about the trade deadline coming up. None of this matters to you. All you can remember is the double David legged out in the first inning, a body-memory that can still feel where your father's hand was while you both jumped up and down while everyone watched and cheered in the stadium as David and ball reached second base at the same time. David slid in head-first. Kenn got the ball and slapped it down for the tag. The umpire waited a second, letting the crowd create its own drama, and swung both arms out to his side. Safe. Now, the other team is trying to pitch around David, but when the ball is hit, the pressure of bat on ball spills out over into the stadium: sounding as if the atmosphere ripped open, finally giving way. And as the ball dive-bombs over the fence, the thundering judgment of the umpire transcends the rising noise of the stadium every time.

This is where you want to tell your father, "I love you." The need to say this makes your legs shake involuntarily: a soft flutter that strangles your stomach and spine. Notice that you now have cotton mouth. Notice your palms are slightly clammy and feel muculent. This is what is meant by "sick with happiness" or maybe it's the cost of being aware that this is "as good as it gets" or maybe this is the commentary to which you submit for a moment of affirmation—a moment of quiet magnificence in a lonely and wrung out year. At this point, everything is suspended: time, the celebratory firework caught in the still moment before it blasts into color, the homerun sign popping on: nothing is wanted but to let your father hear the hysterical and impulsive phrase that's endured absence this last year. But you don't say anything. Too embarrassed to be exposed, too aware of the embarrassment of clichés—the form of played-out emotion in yourself and others—and it's not the fear of him not saying those words back to you that prevents any utterance, but fear that the response won't be felt as deeply as you would want it to be.

You are conscious, mostly, of your inadequacies as a child within a family experienced with loss, the dread of not knowing if what you say will make it worse or not, the lie of trying not to be scared, because you are a child. Plain and simple. Or not. It's complicated. Even at this age, the awareness of raw and vulnerable interactions isn't lost on you. Just enjoy his hand on your shoulder, tightening more and more as David rounds the bases. Like a handshake. Like a vice. You feel there is no need to complicate this moment. When you would ask how long your mother's treatment was at the hospital, your father would tell you that there's a virtue in waiting. And this is your fatal mind-set: you would rather wait. Neither of you understand how the two of you could have saved each other.

Look up. We're winning.

But the other team's momentum can be felt, each pitch thrown from their pitcher has spark and heart, and the infielders jump in place, anticipating whatever will come their way. By the start of the eighth inning, we are losing; it's not even close. A person can't help but feel helpless when they're rooting and playing for the wrong team. And now, behind you, the sun is leaning on the rim of the stadium like a child's head on a mother's shoulder. This is a time in the game when the theatrical suspense present or lack thereof reminds you of the inevitability of the game ending. The stadium is slowly emptying out—strokes of color against the blooming grey palette of the stadium. Concession stands have closed their gates. Vendors call out for last chance treats.

And you turn and mention to your father that you could leave if he was ready.

"We have to see it through 'til the end," he says. "Plus, I need you to look at the scoreboard."

There it is in big, mustard-yellow incandescence, the

words "HAPPY BIRTHDAY" plus your name right below it. The whole scoreboard announcing it's your special
day against the city's expiring day. And here is where there is
laughter and surprise and you hugging your father and people around telling you "Happy Birthday." You are going to
tell your father that you love him, but first he wants to take
your picture. You're holding the bobblehead that looks like me.

Somewhere, mixed in with it all, I meant to get to the
fact that this late summer baseball game, like all late summer
baseball games for teams in last place, doesn't matter—at least
from the perspective of the player. While you stand in front
of your father with no attention paid to the rest of the stadium, unintentionally spilling your perspiring PEPSI cup that
rests on the ground, you'll never know how the game rewards
the whole picture and not the accumulation of small details.
For me, this game is already lost, I've already stopped looking for a way around it. We'll always sacrifice the quality of
today for the quantity of tomorrows. This should be the moment where I discuss the arc of fate or how lives cross. Do you
have any idea the number of people who sat in that same seat?
I won't go into it. For a little boy trying to have a nice day
with his father, today's game probably meant everything: win
or lose. That's something I'll have to keep in mind. Forever.

But now I have to get to the part where you and your father aren't paying attention, him trying to take your picture
with the scoreboard in the background, and I am up to bat
and anticipate something hard, something fast. My bat speed
is not where it was when the season started—fatigue, the dis-
passionate and waning confidence of being in a slump, but I'm

fooled and overanxious and I swing a split-second too early at a slider spinning lyrically in the air, and the trajectory of the ball slices and curves and bends the air around it toward you.

And when it arrives, there's the deadened thud and the collective gasp and then your father cradling your head like a newborn. He is calling for help. No one does anything but stare. The words you hear are formless and dull, not one echoes within your heart. Look at you. This is the tangible pain of hard violence. This is the end of waiting. Soon your face is warm in a strange, vague way like how your mother's shoulder used to feel. Let go. You feel a small vibration at the small of your back, trying to hold you in place. Sit still. Let the vibration run its course until it stops. Even an unstrummed chord has the potential for sounding beautiful.

There's now a floating away to a place where you are overhead and the stadium looks like an open mouth gasping for air, a place where the two circumscribed notions of loss and loneliness don't matter anymore, where you can ask whatever you want to ask and say whatever it is you need to say without having to assert or pretend that your silence is somehow a strength, where you can just let go and be exposed, where you are a child surrounded once again by something deep and warm you don't quite understand.

And while all the stadium watches, there's the long delay, the interruption in time as a few people clasp their mouths to prevent any sound coming from their deep reaches, the bundled link of awe and morbid reality. Everywhere a soliloquy of ceaseless movement, interrupted only by the announcer's still active mic.

"Holy shit," says the announcer.

Stadium personnel are scrambling to remove the replay on the scoreboard. Your afterimage, cycling through the infinite loop of your eventual end, moves its video through me again and again. Reliving every brash impatience to play ball, future-less in stride, tomorrow that seat may be filled with someone new, someone who never noticed the blue dense clouds above the city around them. Somehow we'll get on with the game.

INTO SPRING

Julia Johnson

Winter is my favorite time of year—
not so much the cold, but the comfort
of blankets and hot baths.
Here in this place the season
is difficult to discern.
Bitter the night I arrived,
now the willow outside flourishes.
Inside, there's neither warmth nor chill, so
I wander about the aching ward,
search for the right adjustment.
I shrink beneath an all-season blanket.
Its fibers trap body heat,
yet there's no warmth. Perhaps
the glacier of hospital white on which I lie
absorbs all I'm able to radiate.
And I can't draw a hot bath; any volume
of water is forbidden. So I shower,
look up into the tepid spray, regulated
to prevent scalding. There's wetness,
but it holds no heat, instead
washes over my face,
the exact temperature of tears.

BIRTHDAY POEM IN APRIL

PENELOPE SCAMBLY SCHOTT

From across the street, piercing shouts
of school kids at recess

From my black locust tree, deep lament
of mourning doves

long white bridal bouquets of the locust
not yet in bloom

For seventy-three years I've been married
to this blue, blue sky

A ten-year-old girl hunches under juniper
her skirt pulled over her knees

I could run across Sixth Street and tell her
Look up past the branches

Honey, it gets better   Better and better

THE HOLINESS OF WORDS

BILL BROWN

Soft light on the stairs
coming from window—
if I climb you with my eyes
will a warmth puddle inside

Morning dew on spider webs—
too many to count in a mountain
meadow—teach me the meaning
of *lea—pampa—heath—veldt*

Winter trees, tangle of vines
and fish bones against blue,
you have carpeted the forest
making yourself a nest—loam—
earth—terra-cotta—clunch—kaolin—
marl—taste your words on tongue
and lips, on bark and limbs, in roots

Honey Run, seepage, trickle, bubbling
over rocks, then a stretch of carved
limestone for darters and newts: babbling
that greets the ear or hums too deep
in woodland, taiga, timberland, bush

How many languages have formed you

SMOKE AND MIRRORS

BRANDON FRENCH

You don't know, you just don't know how it was. How could
any of you who were born in the '80s or '90s or after 9/11 know
what the world was like back in 1965? There were no ATMs,
no 7Elevens, no all-night Walgreens or CVS. New York City
was closed up like a goddam six-inch-thick steel bank vault,
and even if you found some dingy little café a rat wouldn't
be caught dead in, peddling burnt coffee and stale donuts on
Avenue C, those Ukrainians weren't going to accept a credit
card or a check for a dollar or even a measly 35 cents for the
cigarette machine, if they had one, which they probably didn't.

That morning there wasn't even a bum I could bum one
from. The whole world was asleep like a nursery of infants in
flannel onesies, except for me freezing to death in the middle
of February in the Lanz floral nightgown my mother had sent
me for Christmas and my ugly green terrycloth bathrobe with
the tomato paste stain.

So there I was, outside my apartment building on Avenue
A, wandering around crying like I'd just escaped from a mental
hospital after I'd had another fight with Max about Lynda in
the middle of the night and stayed up smoking and weeping
until I crushed out my last Marlboro. And when I went to

the underwear drawer in the abandoned dresser we'd hauled upstairs from the street because Max believed in salvaging discardables, the few emergency bucks and even a couple of cigarettes I sometimes kept there were gone. Max had cleaned me out.

How could you even *think* it, you'll probably say, as if a twenty-two-year-old college grad could never get desperate enough to do something immoral, or addictions only afflicted uneducated, homeless bums or movie stars. Or maybe you'll say *what about calling a friend?* But I didn't have any friends at 6 a.m. Sunday morning, and not that many at 10 on Tuesday either, but that's another story. My whole life was about Max back then, my gorgeous, gifted, incendiary Max whose photographs of people laughing, raging, suffering, assaulted my eyes mercilessly, burning through my social indifference like hurled acid.

Back then Max's whole life was about his former fiancée Lynda, who he was probably in bed with by now, in her decrepit, five-floor walk-up on Second Avenue that reeked of garlic and boiled cabbage and had a bathtub in the kitchen. I could picture it in my head, right next to Gem's Spa, a newspaper and magazine and egg cream and *cigarette* store which was closed like every other goddam place of business in Manhattan at 6 a.m. Sunday morning in the middle of February, 1965.

I considered walking over there and yelling up at him, *Max! Maxie!* like Stanley Kowalski in *A Streetcar Named Desire.* But I could imagine him shoving the window open and sticking his big curly head out all red faced and mussed up from sleep and shouting at me to go fuck myself and I didn't want to see him up there with her because it would just make me crazy.

I had only seen Lynda once, when I came with Max to help move his boxes out. He had sent all his things from Berkeley, photography books (he idolized Walker Evans and Garry Winogrand), German philosophy books (especially Wittgenstein), winter clothes and photography supplies and everything he owned except his precious Hasselblad, because he was moving to New York to marry her and she didn't know how to tell him that she'd fallen in love with a Danish actor named Hans. So she and Max were in bed together that first night when Hans came home at 2 a.m. and Max said "What the fuck!" and Lynda began to cry and said "I'm confused." Max moved out the next morning, all broken-hearted and bitter, and a few nights later I met him at Max's Kansas City, official headquarters for all lower Manhattan artists (owned by another Max whose real name was Mickey Ruskin, a Max with money) and the next day moneyless Max moved in with me because he had nowhere else to go, and that's when we went to get all his boxes. But now, a year later, Lynda and Hans were on the outs, and she wanted Max back.

So what am I, chopped liver? I shouted, causing a pair of pigeons to take off like fireworks from a ledge above me. My words splattered the buildings and splashed down onto the street. Two yellow cabs and a bus rolled over them without stopping. Then silence.

I thought I should go upstairs to my apartment. Maybe go back to sleep. At least get dressed. I started to walk uptown, what the hell, maybe I'd find a butt on the sidewalk with a little bit of unsmoked tobacco. Like some bum, I thought, I'm turning into a bum. A man came out of a building, raising up the collar of his jacket and wrapping a scarf around his neck. I walked toward him, hopefully. He looked at me like I was a freak, like maybe I had another head or an extra arm hidden inside my bathrobe.

"Do you have a cigarette?"

He didn't say anything, he just walked past, scowling, keeping his eye on me like he thought I might suddenly knife him in the leg or something, which maybe I would have if I'd had a knife. The *sonofabitch.*

Max was a sonofabitch, too, of course. He insisted I wasn't really his girlfriend – "You're my roommate," he said. "Do you sleep with your roommates?" I yelled. "I don't want to sleep with you," he said, "but there's only one bed." "Fuck you, Max! If I'm only your roommate, then you should pay rent." "Fine, I'll move out," he said, knowing the absolute power of that threat, knowing it would bring me to my knees. "I don't want you to go," I sobbed. "Please don't leave me."

I kept walking. No butts anywhere. Any other day Manhattan was a garbage scow, today it was clean as a hospital operating room.

What am I doing? I asked myself, looking down at my bedroom slippers slapping softly against the pavement like two dead fish. What else is there to do? I answered.

My mother had said to me, "New York is such a lonely city,

why do you want to move to such a lonely place, Christy?" I wanted to tell her, "San Diego is pretty lonely, too, Mom, at least for me," but I knew that would just upset her. She was always encouraging me to "go out and play, why don't you go out and make friends, Christy?" ever since I was a little kid. She couldn't understand why I liked to stay in my room and read novels like *Misty of Chincoteague* or *The Black Stallion,* or build cities with my blocks, populating them with plaster-of-paris people and a lot of horses that I'd created myself. At the time I was convinced that if I only had a horse, I wouldn't need friends.

Tompkins Square Park was as deserted as a bomb site. Two bums were stretched out corpselike on a bench, wrapped up in some murky white canvas that looked like butcher paper. One bum began to scratch his belly without opening his eyes. An empty beer bottle rolled off the bench and landed on the pavement without shattering. I'd had a policy of not giving panhandling drunks money to fuel their addictions, but now that I was in the same boat, I began to reconsider my position.

A guy in a faded blue pea coat appeared out of nowhere and meandered crablike in my direction, studying me as if he was an entomologist and I was a Hercules Beetle. He was unshaven and his unwashed hair was sticking up from his head in stiff points, like stalagmites. He looked around cautiously as if any minute my nark partner would jump out of the bushes and arrest him. *Yes, I'm an undercover nark in a green terrycloth bathrobe,* I thought. What a great disguise.

"What?" he said in a growly voice, like I'd just woke him up.

"Huh?"

"What?" he repeated, screwing up his face so his nose and mouth squished together like a juiced orange.

"Can I bum a cigarette?"

"What do I look like?"

"You look like a smoker."

"What do you *want?*" he asked, enunciating each word like I was retarded. He looked around again and then pulled a baggy out of his pocket, waving it at me slyly. Inside were three joints, nestled together like white worms.

I wasn't tempted. Marijuana had sent me to the Emergency Room with a panic attack the year before.

"I guess we won't be fooling around with weed anymore, right?" the short, sexy intern wearing his stethoscope around his turtleneck like jewelry had said as he injected me with Valium.

No, we certainly won't.

"I want a Marlboro," I told the dealer.

"What do I look like?" he asked again, obviously a man with a limited number of rejoinders.

I didn't want to tell him he looked like a drug peddler because I thought that might spook him. And after all, I didn't exactly look like Princess Grace of Monaco.

"It doesn't have to be a Marlboro, any brand will do," I said, mustering up an ingratiating little smile.

He turned away and spit on the grass.

"Okey-dokey," I said, and began to walk back toward the

bum bench. I thought about waking one of them up if I could get past the smell. You never knew, they might have a couple of butts stashed in a pants pocket.

My lips were dry and cracked from the cold. I ran my tongue over them and felt a longing for the familiar bump of the filter, followed by the first long drag that billowed through my mouth on its merry way down into my lungs. I groaned with desire.

"Dear God," I whispered, as if God in his mercy would reach down from heaven like Michelangelo's *Creation of Adam* and light me up.

An older man with a dark beard and skin the color of baked butternut squash came into the park and walked toward me, his hands jammed into the pockets of his leather jacket for warmth. His eyes were bloodshot and puffy and he looked nervous like he'd just robbed a store. There was something about the way he stared at me that made me feel self-conscious, like I was half-naked instead of half-dressed. I folded my arms protectively across my chest.

"How much?" he mumbled.

No one had ever asked me that question before but I knew what he meant. The awful thing was that I considered how to answer. *A carton of cigarettes? Two cartons?* I wasn't going to sell myself any cheaper than that.

Then I heard my mother's voice. It was even louder and more shrill than usual. And now she was so upset that she was having a hard time forming words. It was like a strangled scream, like "Agggghhhrhrhrhrhrhrh!"

"No thanks," I said, walking away quickly, two bright red

cartons of Marlboros disappearing into the flat white morning light.

I left the park and walked west like an automaton toward 2nd Avenue, a poor brain-washed Laurence Harvey in *The Manchurian Candidate* heading out on a suicide mission. A crumpled Valentine, one of the cheap dime store kind with cute animals that kids gave each other by the dozens, blew past me on its way under the wheel of a vandalized Buick. *Valentine's Day, what a laugh.*

I reached St. Marks Place and parked myself in front of Gem's Spa, looking up five floors to Lynda's apartment—Lynda my rival, with her scraggly, dishwater blond hair and her chipped front tooth and her gangly, meatless body. I was getting ready to yell "Max!" at the top of my lungs when I caught sight of my reflection in the store's murky window. *My God.* Only in New York could someone walk twelve blocks in a nightgown, bedroom slippers and a bathrobe without drawing major attention. It was like the story of the man in the Brooks Bros. suit I'd read about in the *Daily News* who collapsed on Fifth Avenue and people just stepped over him, hurrying on their way uptown.

Who *are* you, I asked my reflection with the spiky hair, sad clown's mouth, and exhausted eyes. *Who the hell is that ridiculous looking beggar in the glass?* Tomorrow I would wake up at 6:30 in the morning, take a shower and get dressed in a Lord & Taylor suit, silk blouse and high heels, as I had done without fail five days a week for the last year-and-a-half, and take the subway uptown to Madison and 59th Street, where I was an advertising media buyer at McElroy and Dodge. How could that same person be standing here now looking back at me like an escapee from Bellevue? And which one was the *real* me?

I thought about the people I'd seen in the last hour, going somewhere, or nowhere, having nowhere to go, or no one to go to, and the excoriating judgments I'd made about them. Maybe every one of them had experienced a moneyless, friendless, desperate Sunday dawn in a locked down, heartless city, maybe an entire year of them, or even a whole lifetime.

I didn't yell up. Maybe Max wasn't even there, I told myself. He might be with his friend Tony in the West Village. That's what he'd say anyway when he got home, and he *would* come home, eventually, because I had all his stuff, including his Hasselblad. I wouldn't question him. What would be the point? He'd have cigarettes, Players, his brand, never my own of course, but I'd smoke them gratefully until Bankers Trust opened tomorrow and I could get some cash. I wouldn't tell him about the dealer in the park who wanted to sell me marijuana or the man who wanted to pay to have sex with me or the fact that I'd seriously considered it because I was so desperate for a smoke, because he'd just look at me like I was a hydrocephalic dwarf spouting gibberish and then he'd walk over to the TV and turn it on extra loud.

I heard a bang, like someone had just slammed a window shut or shot off a gun. I looked around uneasily until I realized that the noise was inside my head. It suddenly occurred to me that I felt the same way about Max as I did about cigarettes. That's when I knew, just as surely as the sun rose up over the East River every morning and set down onto the Hudson each night, that sooner or later they'd both probably kill me if I didn't give them up.

KINDRED

KIM GARCIA

The hand at work, the heart's drone,
mind-dance in honeycomb. The path

of flower, clover song, sweet cellulitic
bubbling magma, cooled in stone. River

rock's tumbling wash, a karst of blue.
A sky mountainous with frowning cloud,

stars slipping the city's hot gaze, fastening
their new eyes over fresh yearnings,

drawn up along the lines of the old ache
like desert seed, fashioning green tongues.

JOSEPH CORNELL ON THE PRAIRIE

Michael Estes

Barn be red, barn be black
and blue from threshing, barn

at least be closed. The sun
is judge, jury and colt

in a wide field and doesn't ask
to run. When it jumps

a fence it leaves a taste
of cake from three counties

over to see if the fence will
follow. Some gray flakes of fence

have fallen and gone
and the sun gives what's left

a dry rough tongue
to speak. For awhile it just talks

about wind. Then clapboard stripped,
birds in heat and how good

it felt to let the weeds in
the first time. It starts

to list the names it has
for the horizon, and the sun bolts

to make a cherry of the west.
The fence and the barn both

know the sun has never taken
no for an answer, and they're considering

an installation. Nothing big,
just a roof, be it golden, be

it amber, be it somehow
here for good.

OLD DOG, OLD TRICKS
(A BIRDER'S APOLOGY)

GAYLORD BREWER

Oh, maybe a dozen years ago
    I came slogging up the same slick hill
        in the Central Valley,
      mashing through these banana palms

and coffee bushes on a foul
    afternoon, tracking a Squirrel Cuckoo
        among the shadows of leaves,
      a lovely bird as wet as I was.

Anyone with sense was in her casita
    napping or with a pot of tea.
        Now a man nearly fifty traipsing
      the same damned property, 6:40 a.m.,

no lesson learned and no
    danger except landing on my ass.
        The sun's out, it's hot already,
      and this entirely my neighbor's fault

with tall tales of her hearing twice
    at dawn the frog-like *ribbet ribbet*
        of a Keel-Billed Toucan's throaty
      whisper. Yesterday afternoon,

in the rain, yes, I'd stalked a pair of shy
   yet teasing Blue-Crowned Motmots—
     I kid not—couldn't get enough
    of comical tip of tail feather,

iridescent blue crest, black eyemask.
   And not to brag, *three* Great Kiskadees
     Monday, one at the fountain
    if you believe it. So, still the greedy,

grinning fool after half a century,
   returned to the quest, sweating
     my shirt, glasses fogged, breath oddly
    even, feeling almost good, almost—

alright, damn it—happy. What chance
   do dark verses have, my induced
     and near-famous angst? I flush a
    White-Tipped Dove, spook a Brown Jay

noshing berries. Humming-
   birds swooshing, and not one dream
     of despair, or even a credible
    hangover, as reward for the night.

ALL THE WORLD SAILS TO HOUTHAVEN

ALLISON ALSUP

They were coming back from the Saturday market where in addition to buying bread, fish and sausages, his mother had purchased two small bunches of daffodils. Frans was only eight; still he knew the flowers were frivolous. His mother could wait one more month and pick a bouquet from the small garden behind their house.

Buying the flowers was the third strange thing his mother had done that morning. The first was that she had put on her good green church coat, not her everyday brown. The second was that she'd told Frans' younger brother he was not to come to the market but stay at home and mind their older sisters. Jan had cried though Frans was secretly pleased; he knew his mother would buy a raisin bun at the baker's stall, and now he wouldn't have to share it. Then came the daffodils, the third strange thing.

So when Frans turned towards their street and she reached for his collar, saying, *Not yet,* it was simply the fourth. He wondered if more strange things were yet to come.

He followed behind her skirts, carrying the still warm bread and content to follow whatever errand if it kept him from having to sit at home. His fingers were sticky from the raisin bun. He'd finished it quickly in case she changed her mind and made him save half for Jan. He watched her boot heels click against the cobblestones. He could see where she'd tried to cover the scuffs with black to make them look new again. It did not do, she said, for a housekeeper not to be kept. If there was money to spend at the baker's stall, it came from what his mother earned sweeping, washing and ironing at the doctor's house Mondays and Thursdays.

The air smelled of wet leaves and brine from the harbor. The port was close by; their neighborhood, Houthaven, was named for it. Frans' father worked there as the head patrolman. When Frans and Jan walked along the strand on the way to school and then on the way home, they often saw their father in his blue woolen coat and cap, helping to guide the massive hulls through the fog. Papa would raise his thick hand to wave, and Frans would raise his own. For a moment it was as if he too, were on the boats. But his father did not work Saturdays, and so Frans had no reason to wave.

As he trailed his mother, Frans listened to the green water slap against the pier. Like water, he could not be still. Like water, he would one day go everywhere. He thought about it even when he knew he shouldn't—in the church pew or in class where his teacher scolded Frans for bobbing his legs under his desk and knocking his slate to the floor. His mother told him that even as a baby, his hair had grown in like his father's— burnished from the sun and curled into stiff locks by salty spray. It was as if Frans were already a sailor before he'd left the brackish wash of his mother's womb.

Now he watched the rocking ships and imagined which

trade winds had filled their sails before Amsterdam or what freight waited below in the holds. He imagined where the boats might go next: Bristol, Greenland, the Caribbean, Cape Horn, the Dutch East Indies—all the places Papa had seen as a young sailor. At supper each night, their father described the marvelous things he'd seen that day: Chinese silks and Moroccan leather, Indian spices and Javanese coffee.

Once I sailed the world, their father often told them, lifting his finger like a preacher. *But now all the world sails to Houthaven!*

Of course, Papa also had sea stories of his own: tales of bright birds and gold coins, of amber-skinned women and barnacled whales that raced the prow. Once Frans asked his father if he missed the sea, and his father said yes, very much, but that there comes a time when a man must choose: be a good sailor or a good papa. One could not be both.

Frans was about to ask his mother if he could chew one end of the bread, when they reached the edge of the cemetery. She wove through the stones towards the back wall where it was shaded and the headstones grew soft with moss. Wordlessly she put down her basket and placed the yellow flowers in the small stone cup in front of a tombstone. Frans had never been to the graves before. He wondered what he and his mother were doing there. He knew it wasn't right to eat, not even a crust, in a graveyard.

"You can read it, yes?" she asked, laying her arm across his shoulder and pulling him against the swell of her hip.

Frans looked closer at the stone and saw the name was his

own. *Meijer.* He thought of those they'd left just the hour before: Jan, and their sisters, Maria and Alida. He shook his head, slipping from his mother's grasp. It had to be a trick, a terrible trick.

"Calm yourself," she said. "You didn't know them. Look." She pointed at the pair of dates and he saw: just one day separated them. It had happened before Frans was born. Otherwise the marker was plain and small.

"Your brothers," she explained. "It was very quick. The fever took them. Papa almost died himself."

It was the first Frans had ever heard of the two boys. He could see from the dates that they wouldn't have been old enough to go to the market or carry the bread.

"Papa never told me," he said, as if a thing could be true only if his father had spoken it.

"No. Papa doesn't talk of it," his mother told him. "When the fever came, he sent me and your sisters away. I did not want to leave, but he said I had to, for me and the girls, to keep us safe from the fever. So we stayed with your aunt. Papa was right. There was nothing we could have done."

"But Papa lived."

"Yes. The good doctor saved him. And God, of course."

Her eyes closed as she grasped the small silver cross at her neck.

Frans did not understand why God would choose to save his father and not his brothers, and then he had another thought, one that made better sense. "Now it is like before, the same number with me and Jan," he said, proud of having done the sums backwards, 4-2, and then forwards, 2+2, as he'd learned in school.

She pressed his hand tightly, before letting go. Her thin smile did not last. "Yes. Four children. Two daughters, two sons."

Frans understood. He and his brother were replacements, like new boots when the old ones have broken beyond repair. It wasn't that he and Jan weren't loved. But if the other two boys had survived, Frans and his brother would not need to exist. He asked why there was only one stone for two children.

"A stone is expensive," she explained. "Papa could not work for quite some time after. It was very hard."

"But you said the doctor made him better."

"It was very hard, Frans," she repeated. She swallowed and reached into her pocket for her handkerchief. "You see, Papa was sick first. He brought the fever, a foreign sickness from the boats."

"When he was still a sailor?"

"Yes."

Frans pictured his father coming home from the port, a loaf of bread tucked under his arm like the one Frans held now, only Papa's loaf was black. His father had brought the black bread home. But of course, it wouldn't have been like that. The sickness was hidden, an invisible cargo. It had never occurred to Frans the boats held dangerous things that even his father, whose sharp eyes could spot trap doors and trick panels, couldn't see.

"There was no way for him to know," his mother said, "but Papa could not forgive himself. Even now."

She took the bread from Frans' arms and laid it on the

basket before bending at the knees and turning Frans to face
her. Her handkerchief hung rumpled from her fist and her hair
was starting to slip from its knot. He knew the stray locks
would bother her if she saw them. She was always reminding
Frans and especially Jan, who was forever forgetting his tin
soldiers on the kitchen table, *A thing left out today means more
work put in tomorrow.*

"It is why we can say nothing of our little trip here," she
said, gripping Frans' arms to keep him from shifting. "There
are things you will understand more when you are older, but
know that when your father is sad, he is very, very sad. There is
nothing to be done except wait for the dark clouds to pass."

Frans already understood. Sometimes his father did not rise
for work, like just before the Christmas holiday when Frans
had come home from school and discovered the door to his
parents' room ajar. Peering through the dark slice, he saw the
white of his father's nightshirt lying on the mattress, his body,
save his face, lost to the twisted sheets. His mother had found
Frans standing in the hall. *Papa is sleeping,* she said, pulling the
door shut. But Frans knew Papa was not sleeping. His father's
eyes had been open and staring. It was as if his father did not
see his own son standing there, as if there were something
floating over Frans' head. A ghost, a flag. Frans knew he was
not to mention such days. He now wondered if Papa's fever,
though long gone, had left something worse behind to take its
place.

Frans moved between his legs, pressing on one foot then
the other, anxious to walk again. He wanted to leave the
graveyard and for his mother to stop weeping and looking at

the stone. It was too late to ask about the bread crust, and his nose had started to run from the cold. He told her he would carry both her basket and the bread. He was strong and could be trusted; he would not drop them.

She nodded, her eyes ringed with red. "We'll mention nothing of where we've been, not to Papa or your sisters. Understand? Jan is too little to know. This is just between us. A secret."

Suddenly she tilted and reached for his shoulders. Though his legs screamed to move, he managed to stand very still until she steadied herself.

"You are different from the rest, Frans. Already a little man, so much like your father. It's why I've brought you, so that you will understand. You will remember our secret, yes?"

"Yes," he replied, although she'd said so many things, he wasn't sure what he was supposed to understand or which part was the secret.

She tucked her handkerchief back into her coat, then bending at the waist, pulled up a clump of weeds and tossed them to the side. "They never cut the grass as short as they should," she said and weaved her way towards the street.

Years later when Frans worked as a hand in the experimental section of the botanical garden, he remembered his father's words. *All the world sails to Houthaven.* Indeed for a time, they seemed true. Nearly every week, crates and seed bags arrived at the gates from across the oceans, and on occasion, sunburned, spectacled men whose calloused fingers clutched glass Wardian cases too precious to entrust to anyone else with their delivery:

rare, quivering orchids, blossoms like Chinese lanterns, avocado seeds shaped like wooden eggs. As he worked in the loamy heat of the exotic greenhouse, Frans sometimes remembered the small headstone or pictured the black bread, and yet he planted and watered and pruned the foreign plants without fear. Longing for the taste of distance, was often the first to suck from a red, warty fruit or bite into an oily black nut.

Weekends he took to walking miles and miles to the coast in order to watch the waves break over the sand. Everything seemed larger there than at home: the sea, the ships, the horizon. Turning his back to the rented wicker chairs and taffy sellers, he imagined he could see the green hump of England waiting across the water. He was seventeen, old enough. His mother fretted he would catch sick or be swept away. *Always walking. Always eating oats from your pockets like a cart horse! You are too thin, Frans.*

He laughed, not cruelly, only to quiet her. It was not dangerous, he assured her; the North Sea was much too cold for swimming. He said he slept behind the flood wall though often he did not. He could not explain that he *had* to walk, how his legs demanded the miles, how only exhaustion scattered the clouds that had begun to gather. Nor did he tell her that one day soon he would not return. He would either cross the sea or walk into it. It was not as Papa said. All the world did not sail to Houthaven.

Sundays when he came back to the narrow house, sometimes after supper, always having missed church, he would quietly slip through the blue door and step down the hall, avoiding the boards that creaked. He knew he would find his mother waiting in the kitchen, seated at the long table with the remains of the soup pot warming over the fire and the last of the bread wrapped in a cloth. His father would already be sleeping or pretending to. Often Maria and Alida, who like their mother now swept, washed and ironed for money, sat beside her. If he were very quiet, Frans could stand for several minutes, simply watching them as they knitted or darned and talked of dress buttons or pastry crusts or complained of how their hair refused to hold a curl, before suddenly clapping his hands and making them jump. *Gossiping again?* he might call out, *Stealing the last of the apple cake?*

But if she were alone, his mother would detect even the quietest steps. Rising, she would wrap him in her shawl and lean her head against the shallows of his chest. Once when he was very late, she raised her arm and slapped him.

Why must you wander so far, Frans? she pled, the tears welling. *Why?*

He did not have the heart to tell her of the invisible cargo he now carried in the dark holds of his mind.

SOLSTICE

Ruth Williams

Weather like
warm wallpaper,
smack of a slick back
onto chest, arms,
enveloping the body
until it blends
into summer's pattern:
light, not light. So
one could imagine
glossy tethers in our dark hair—no
crown of flowers,
something more
fierce, light hooked
to position heads. Uncanny
how the white of it makes
everything both
more defined—sharper—
and more painful,
so we find
our eyes reined in,
viewing things askance,
never fully knowing

what faces us, yet
feeling assured
by the shadows that
something is there.

SISTERS, WE MUST HARDEN OUR OWN HONEY

Ruth Williams

In French, a verb can be forced into the active form
with the application of -*ant*. So outside, snow falls,
inflamed cells in need of cooling—*ant, ant.*

No more of grandfather's honey to dapple, to glen.
Soured, our aunt's cancered guts strain her stitched stomach.
A long tube of oxygen floats through the room.

Somewhere warmer a man charms a snake, makes it sit up,
beg for air. To lift our aunt from the toilet, my grandmother
wedges herself tight in a small wooden chair.

Gathering the dappled intestine
like a beehive juicy with snakes, we all harden,
preserve a mordant honey.

But I want to be on fire in the bees' glen. Then,
the firemen would be taken with me. Flumed with emergency
in the apple core time of winter.

Decay, that red elbow of pain indwelling:
an inheritance, a natural correspondence.
Some unholy *ant* inside us.

ROUGHNECK

Harris Lahti

After a minor search, I find the Folgers in the cabinet next to the Pop-Tarts, and despite it being forbidden by Rule Three on the list Wade's magneted to the refrigerator, I also take a Pop-Tart. On the piece of computer paper, his handwriting is medium-sized and official-looking but becomes increasingly cramped towards the bottom where additional rules have been made and amended. Squinting, I carefully peel the Pop-Tart's silver-foil wrapper then I chew with my mouth shut.

Rule Seven decrees: Unplug Power Strip Before Putting Coffee On. And today I decide to honor this rule despite a nearly overwhelming impulse not to do it at all—even if the breaker is certain to pop and kill the electric to my essential space heater. The back porch—where I live—is a thin square of storm windows and particle board with no insulation or electric to speak of. With the recent cold snap, I'm barely getting by on a jerry-rigged power strip I snake under the door. But even so, all that considered, still, I have a knee-jerk impulse to say no—no, I will not unplug the power strip—just because Wade took the time to put the list up there, telling me not to, like I'd forget.

The coffee maker gurgles and chokes off a series of black

drips that plink into the dead center of the glass pot. I notice some grinds on the counter and fleck them to the floor with the edge of my hand. I think, you're welcome, Wade.

When Wade's not pouring over his textbooks or drinking coffee like it's beer, he's a practicing Swiffer Grand Master. A decorated bombardier general of tidiness, in fact. In a lot of ways, there's philanthropy in my messiness. If it weren't for me, there would be no more dirt left to get. No more practice. Then his skills would dissolve and he'd get out-dusted somewhere down the line. No kidding.

He's an aspiring paleontologist, my brother. Somebody over at the college lets him head a dig on the floodplains out in Schoharie over summers. Wade invited me out once, and my ex Katherine insisted we go. I remember Wade wore this dumb hat—think Indiana Jones turned rice famer—and was wildly excited to give us the tour of the worksite's few shallow holes. At least at first, because not two minutes in, one of his crane-necked underlings unearthed something and all hell broke loose. After that Wade basically forgot we were there. But the mosquitoes sure didn't. Those suckers were billowing off the Mohawk River in bloodthirsty clouds. Turned out the excitement was over an ancient Indian bead. It only really looked like a pebble to me, but who am I to say? Wade wouldn't even let me hold it.

When the coffee is done, I go and call up to Wade's office— which is really only the attic—and of course, his answer is, "What?" because did I mention my voice is totally useless? Especially in the mornings, but mostly always. Useless. It's not from the boozing or smoking or singing along with "vocally abrasive" lyrics, either, like you might think. It's just how I was born, with a voice as gruff as a gargoyle's. My brother got brains, and I a mouthful of marbles. But Rule Nine does state: Inform Wade Whenever Fresh Pot Is Done, so I clear my throat and try again. This time he answers.

"Coffee? Yes please," he says. "Just make sure you unplug the power strip," but then I hear his feet pounding toward the stairs like I'm going to forget the power strip anyway. Wade will stay up for days, sequestered in the attic, thumbing books and grinding his teeth away on Adderall.

When Wade enters the kitchen, he's pale as lemon sherbet with these bloodshot eyes, and as I aim a cup of coffee into his quaking hands, I can't help but note the bewildering similarity between our skin tones. Turns out, between the little gaps in my tattoos, I'm pale milk-toast pale, too. It's cause for alarm, really.

People always say we're identical, my brother and me. But people say a lot of things, and I never saw it. You could also say he's squintier, also. Picture somebody who's been reading small print in the dark for too long. "I've been worried about you," he tells me after a long gulp of black coffee. "What was all that yelling about last night?"

That yelling: Night before my cell phone rang, and out of the blue, here comes Katherine back into my life. Her voice sounded like somebody rushing to a hospital bed: *"Harold, what happened!?"*

"If you don't know already, you wouldn't be calling," I

had told her—and I was going to leave it there, but then she baited me with her silent act and I started up again. "Well if you're going to be a ghoul about it, yes, it all happened exactly like you've undoubtedly heard. I almost killed the geezer. Guy that old had no business working security at Price Chopper in the first place. Thought he had World War Two muscles. Spry enough to call me a "punker," but too old and fragile to deal with the repercussions. His badge was barely laminated and he swung first. Yes, Katherine, it's true. I beat the elderly—"

"Don't joke like that," she told me—Katherine was always trying to teach me jokes worked differently for girls, how she wasn't one of my dumbshit friends. We'd been working on that. But it wasn't her place anymore. However before I could set her straight, she added, "I still care about you, Harold…" just like that. I still care. But that was the other thing: Katherine cared about everything and everybody. It pissed me off. There was no hierarchy in her heart. Nevertheless, hearing these words, it set off some wildly romantic impulse. I thought some miracle was occurring. "There's that place down on Central," I heard myself saying. "The Italian one you always talked about—"

"Harold, please…" was all she said.

And let me tell you, hearing that: I've had my fair share of experiences with LSD and Magic Mushrooms, but there's nothing as hallucinogenic as the emotion of jealousy. Because right then, when she declined my offer, it was too much to bear. I saw that other man. An image of them materialized right there before me. Him: whispering in her other ear while rubbing her shoulders in support her of Holy kindness. Her: shushing him with pink cheeks. I saw it all too clearly. There wasn't a doubt in my mind. I couldn't help shouting out: "Who the fuck is there with you!?"

But of course, I tell my brother none of this. If I tried, the words wouldn't come out right. All he'd hear is a blender pureeing wet hamburger. Nobody on Planet Earth except Katherine could ever understand a word out of my mouth the first time around without cupping their ears. So I keep it simple. I tell him, "Nothing at all," but even this is too garbled.

"I'm sorry, Harold. I didn't catch that," he says.

"Nothing, Wade."

"What?"

"*Poopoo caca,*" I say.

"Uh-huh," he replies absently, noticing the coffee grinds. "I see."

Digging in the closet for the Swiffer, Wade asks if I'm planning on going out today, if that's what I'm doing. "News said it's going to be nice out for a change," he says, wiggling his eyebrows, trying to sell me on the idea. Like he's doing me a favor. Then he slides the Swiffer over the coffee grinds and takes a moment to marvel in his favorite toy's efficiency. "Well?" he says. "Would you like some company?"

And that's when I realize Wade's worried I'm going to skip bail. I can't remember the last time he's willingly left the house, the attic for that matter. What kind of derelict does he think I am? Skipping bail. Screw his thousand bucks, I think. I'm skipping bail! I'll show him to make assumptions.

But then I count to ten, like Katherine used to say, and when I finish counting, I manage a shrug and affect if not brotherly love, at least brotherly tolerance. It actually works, too, the counting. Then, before I can even finish shrugging, Wade downs the rest of his coffee and says, "Just let me grab my coat. I need some smokes, anyway," and I have to start counting again.

Snowmelt is gushing in little rivers through the gutters down the slope of Madison Avenue toward the Hudson River. You couldn't even step off the curb if you were seven-feet tall and lanky, it's so rapid.

As we walk with the current toward the Stewart's, my brother jabbers about the Tulip beds, which, as mucky as they are, have already sprouted a few green hairs. Tulipa gensneriana, he calls them. "This is why you got beat up in high school," I tell him, but he doesn't catch a word. He's roving ahead like a dog.

At the counter at Stewart's, a lip-ringed girl in a maroon collared-shirt sells my brother three packs of Camel Cigarettes and a thirty-two ounce coffee which he drinks most of before paying. She looks a little like Katherine, around the blue eyes. "How much for a strawberry milkshake?" I ask her. When she cocks an ear at me, I say, "Never mind," but then she cocks the other ear.

Outside by the ice machine, Wade shucks out two cigarettes. When the smoke hits my throat, it knocks some gravel loose, and I double-over coughing. "Are you okay," Wade asks, reaching for my shoulder.

At his touch, I straighten out, take a smaller, more

cautionary drag, and blow smoke in his face to show him that, Yes, I'm okay. But even this he doesn't seem to understand.

Here Wade's face grows concerned and I begin to fear he might attempt to do something personal. Something like: *No, Harold, how are you really doing? How are you adjusting to life sans Katherine, with the possibility of jail looming in the future, living with me, your mildly autistic brother?* Instead, all he does is take another gulp of coffee and start talking about the extinction of the dinosaurs. "They didn't go extinct like they say, you know," he says. "It wasn't a meteor strike that did it at all. Leading paleontologists theorize that it was a lack of a taste aversion that killed them off, that since the dinosaur biology likely lacked the mechanism to properly differentiate between what was safe to eat and what was poisonous, the herbivores probably feasted endlessly on poisonous vegetation without having the sense to spit it out. They never learned to avoid it, Harold! That's the point. It made them toxic. And then the carnivores ate them up, in turn poisoning themselves, and so on and so forth, until the poison had worked its way entirely up the food chain, until there was nothing left but bones." He says that last bit like it didn't happen a million years ago, like it only happened yesterday. Then he takes a deep pull from his cigarette, and continues, "But human's are different," he says. "Along with insight and self-awareness, they have a taste aversion…" and this is where I lose him. We walk.

As Wade prattles on, I see a crack, another crack, a crumpled beer can and an oblong puddle with a knotted used-condom settled at the bottom. A dad and his kid in church garb are coming up the sidewalk, and as they pass the dad touches his son. A protective impulse, I realize. This is why people never let me pet their dogs or goo-goo their babies, I think. This must be why Katherine left me. Then Wade's touching me again. "Do you understand, Harold?" he says. "Do you see what I'm saying?"

"Yes, Wade, I see what you're saying."

"Good," he says. "I'm glad. That's important, Harold. It's crucial to be able to make these connections. It's what makes us Homo sapiens. Wise Men…"

Passing an old gabled church, I notice a gas-puff of graffiti on its white clapboard siding. There are more tulip beds. Up ahead, a CDTA bus stops at a depot for a tattered-looking woman who doesn't acknowledge the bus in the slightest. And then Wade's doing it again: he's touching me, touching me and wagging his gigantic coffee cup in my direction.

"Harold," he says. "I have to pee."

A bag in the wind, an urban tumble weed. A cloud moves across the bright midday sun. I shrug.

"I have to pee," he says again, staring at me now.

"I know," I say, slowing to a stop. "I heard you."

At this, he scratches his bald spot at me. "Harold, I really have to urinate and I'm beginning to worry."

Here's where I throw my hands up and start back up toward the apartment, but he's frozen in place and doesn't follow. "I'll never make it," he calls.

When I turn, his eyes are darting around for a public bathroom.

"It's Sunday," I tell him. "Nothing happens in Albany on Sunday besides Church and Brunch." He doesn't compute though, only the bald spot again, more scratching. "Fine," I say, "uh, okay, that's where I'd go," and I point to the closest alleyway.

At first his look is skeptical. Then, to my surprise, off he goes at a waddle. I couldn't help feeling a small measure of satisfaction at that. For a moment, I consider leaving him there, wedged in there between the brick wall and the dumpster, but something about the way his head keeps darting over his shoulder turns me soft. Back in high school, Wade used to refuse to use the public facilities out of pure stage fright, and apparently he hasn't overcome that particular anxiety.

"I can't go," he informs me. "Not here, at least."

Then after he teaches me the word *paruresis*—"the intense fear of public urination"—the whole thing turns into this episode of Goldilocks and the Three Bears: this spot's too public, there's a cat staring at me from the window, the dumpster behind Jewel of India smells like a corpse. "You'd never understand," he tells me as we approach a co-ed in slippers out on her stoop. When I ask her if we can use her bathroom and tell her it was a *paruresis*-type emergency, she tells me that her dog is vicious. "Straight Cujo," I think were her words.

"We could've been home already," I try to tell him, but even if I had the voice of an angel, Wade wouldn't understand. He's completely deaf from pressure in the bladder. All he wants to do is waddle. You take him away from a book or his funny hat, my brother's a complete infant.

The whole thing drags on for hours...well, okay, maybe not hours, but at least long enough for me to start losing my patience. It has its limits, you know, just like anything—a bladder, a prison sentence, a relationship, the universe. And wouldn't you know it? Right as I'm about to pull the plug and abandon ship, right as my patience meter's tilting dangerously deep into the red, Wade finds some inspiration.

"There," he says wistfully, as if he's found all-salvation. In the distance, a small park has just reared up like some oasis. There's an alcove of square hedges with a monument poking out. On the flag pole, old glory is cracking in the wind.

"Right behind you," I say, and then, for whatever reason, I think to add, "Little brother," which is something I haven't done in a long time, which is also something I wouldn't be surprised to find outlawed in the smaller print of Wade's list of rule. It's something he's always hated, something that's always worked him like a well-placed kidney shot.

"You're three minutes older than me!" he shouts over his shoulder, the exertion causing him to wince. I grin, satisfied. He waddles, stops. Waddles again. "Let's just get this over with," he says, with his careful mincing steps. He's basically hula-hooping trying to keep the urine in. When we reach the mouth of the square hedges, however, he stops short. "Oh, no," he says.

I crane over his shoulder and see, across from a bronze statue of a solider shouldering a rifle, a bum sleeping on the granite bench with an empty shopping cart at his duct-taped shoes. Good Will attire, a pilly beanie, fingerless gloves, even a little cardboard sign scrawled in a desperate handwriting—he's as chiseled a representation of his kind as the bronze solider, this guy. A real Ironweed. By the looks of him, too, he's down

for the count. Maybe even dead—but hey, I'm no doctor. Nor
a detective. The scene does speak for itself: the empty shopping
cart says it all—A payday. Five-cents a can can get a guy enough
SKOL to get warm and enough heroin to get well, nod out,
sleep like the dead or actually be dead.

Wade looks at the bum and then back at me.

"Yes, Wade. I see," I say. And I do see: I see that this is
getting ridiculous and that something must be done, the pained
look Wade's giving me. So I go over and poke the bum right in
the breast pocket of his wool trench coat, and when I look up,
I make a throat-slashing motion.

"He's dead?" says Wade.

"Yes, Wade, definitely dead," I nod. "Doornail status."

And for whatever reason this seems to soothe him. My trick
works, I guess, because Wade goes over to the corner and
assumes the position, then I see his shoulder's drop at least four
inches and he breathes out in a whoosh. When I hear his
stream, I'm almost proud.

"It feels good to help," Katherine used to always tell me.
And it does. It feels good to help. I'm smiling. An itchy sour-
acid happiness fills my belly, like my insides have licked a nine-
volt battery. I'm not sure if I like this. But I guess Wade's feeling
the love too. It's not too bad actually. I'm smiling. He's smiling
also, and I'm like, Yes, this is what it's all about. Helping a
brother out. Not too bad at all. But would you believe it if I
told you that right then, when the moment was getting nice
and fuzzy and warm, a blur of something crouched and
uniformed on a bike rides by? A cop, I realize.

When I hear the skid, immediately, I know we have a

problem on our hands. I mean, let's analyze the situation here: disregard my track-record with the law, disregard my overall appearance, and it still adds to trouble. Just give a bored cop enough to pick at—look at Wade zipping up, look at the bum, and that's already enough to raise suspicions, enough to pick into a wound, a conflict, a charge. To set me off and send me to jail, definitely and prematurely.

"Morning, Officer," Wade says. But the cop doesn't respond. He just stands there, leaving us to soak in his mustached presence. He's young, for sure. A rookie, no doubt. Looks bored and small, but works out small, like he's a big presence trapped inside a small one, and instead of growing up, he grew out, wide with his muscled arms built for restraining. I can see our bended reflection in the curvature of his police-issued aviator sunglasses.

As he looks us over, I keep my hands in sight and attempt to exude the thoughts of an honest American citizen. I think things like: apple pie, rock and roll, country and hip hop music. I think taxes, paying taxes. I think of tits, ass, domestic beer and Bush—but not pubic bush. George Bush, Jr., and Jeb, Bush. I think of late-night television, toaster ovens, and the Model-T Ford. But no such luck. When the cop finally speaks, the tone is all off and it's to ask us for our IDs. I manage a smile as I remove my ID from my wallet.

When the cop asks us if we're enjoying the weather, I try to let Wade answer. But when he does, the cop tells him to shut it. "I'm not talking to you," the cop says, swinging his sunglasses at me.

"Have anything to drink today?" he asks, to which I shake

my head no. "You know that guy?" he says, signaling to the bum. No. "Any warrants?" No. "Oh yeah?" Yeah. We go on like that for awhile, me answering each of his questions like I'm deaf, dumb, and American. And it's surprising, his response, because in the end, he actually seems satisfied.

Then it's Wade's turn—Wade who's already ingested a heavy dose of Adderall and Caffeine, Wade who's smoked countless cigarettes, Wade with the genius so focused in books and bones that the surrounding world has been rendered entirely unpredictable. His hands shake so bad it'd take him a half-hour to thread a needle. This isn't out of the cop's realm of observation, either. "You're shaking uncontrollably," he says.

"Indubitably," answers Wade.

That's when the cop decides to run our identification. He bends his mouth to the hand-radio on his shoulder and relays the contents of our IDs back to the station in an incomprehensible string of letters and code. Then, all of a sudden, he looks back up. Here it comes, I think. "Twins?" he says. "You're twins?"

"Yes, identical," says Wade nonchalantly, already reaching for his ID.

But the cop swings the ID out of reach and glowers at him—or at least tries to, because, try as he does, there seems to be opposite polarities between their eyes. Wade cannot make eye contact. "Don't see it," says the cop finally.

"Can we go now?" Wade asks the ground.

By way of an answer, the cop begins toying with Wade's ID.

"Please don't do that," Wade says.

"Need to test the integrity of the identification. New York

State mandate," the cop says, mastering a U-shape with the ID. "Got a problem with that?"

And, of course, Wade takes this literally because sarcasm is a foreign idea to my brother. "Yes, as a matter of fact, I do..." he says, erupting into a frenzy of words that I cannot follow. There are a few keywords and phrases that I manage to catch, though. Words like: Forth Amendment and Police Brutality and Ferguson, Missouri, then some references to New York State Statutes and the English Common Law, then something else I'm fairly certain is Latin. But all in all, I have to say, I have no idea what he's saying. However, there's no doubt in my mind that if you slowed his lecture down to an eighth of the speed and gave me three weeks, I'd discover that his words were wrapped together tightly with a jaw-dropping coherence and intellect, that he spoke the truth. Kid's a true genius.

When the cop tells Wade to shut up, I'm not surprised, and Wade does so willingly, expecting the advent of some sportsmanlike discussion. At this point, the cop is as confused as I am, and like most authority figures, when presented with something as bizarre as Wade's intellect or my rough appearance, his options are limited. So he unsheathes a long black flashlight and hoists it to his shoulder, then proceeds to chase Wade's eyes with the beam. "Hold still," he says.

When the cop tries cupping his bald spot for stability, Wade's hands shoot up in self-defense. And that's when the cop deploys his swift take-down maneuver.

Prone with the cop's knee in the small of his back, the fear wipes my brother's face paler than ever, and when he looks at me, it only gets worse. "Don't," he says in a whimper. And that's when I notice that my hands have been replaced with fists. But it's too late. I'm already remembering the too many times I've witnessed this—my brother's face pushed into mud, his glasses broken, pee in his pants, nose bleeding, his backpack inside out and used as a soccer ball, his knees scraped, weak and wobbling, chipped teeth, whimpering, wailing, pleading, bleating and blubbering—and I just can't take it. That's my brother, man! My twin, my roommate since day one! "Get off him, Copper," I say.

But the cop only seems amused by this. "Not a mute after all, eh?" he laughs. "Please, repeat that."

I take a step closer. "I said, *get off*."

"Just wait your turn," the cop says, pointing a finger at me like a gun. "You're next." I half expect him to make a *Pachoo! Pachoo!* sound.

"But he didn't doing anything," Wade cries into the marble floor.

The cop's already drifting too far into Dirty-Harry Land—he makes his voice low and mean, and feeds me the mandatory one-liner: "Nothing talks like that but a weed-whacker or a meth-head," he says, "and I don't see no damn pull-start."

Oh, man! What a line. I can't help but want to laugh at a line like that. I want to just open my mouth and blast him with a laugh, a line like that. But that's the worst kind of thing you can do to a cop—to anyone who's trying to be taken seriously, for that matter—and I know it. But what option do I have? I'm too primed to care. Aren't I?

Of all things, Wade's list on the refrigerator comes to mind, and I find myself wondering what it might say about this given situation, what instructions I might find written there. As I wonder this, I look at my brother lying there on the concrete, and would you believe it if I told you that he answered me without moving his lips? Sure, there are identical twins that share cosmic connections, twins that finish each other's sentences, twins separated at birth who grow up strangers but both name their dog's Scruffy or drive the same car, twins whose neurons transmit and receive information in ways that defy science, but Wade and I have never experienced anything like that. Never once up until this moment, at least, because now, suddenly, all at once, it's happening, and I get it. I turn to the cop and speak as softly as possible, my voice barely modulating or rasping. What do I say? I keep my words short, sweet, and logical. I patiently go through the sequence of events that led us here and explain the situation. I reason. I implore to the cop's sense of humanity and kindness. "Sundays must get pretty boring down here," I tell him. I tell him a lot of things, and he listens. He actually hears me. When his eyebrows crest above his sunglasses, that's how I know.

WHEN WISDOM TURNS HER/HIMSELF
TO A DUSK-WINGED BIRD OF PREY
JEANNE LARSEN

King Nestor knows Telemachus for the protégé of a god. Invites
him [goes the story] to the rope-net bed of a spearman with a rep:
his young own son. Peisistratus drives the chariot; Telemachus
aches to learn who he is. In a buddy-flick roadtrip rhapsody [IV],
the 2 go see those happy heteros, Mr. & Mrs. Menelaus. *Slut that
I was,* says [we're told] Helen. Slips all a drug to kill for a while
their griefs. To gawky Telemachus, comes on. Brags of bathing
on [a lie?] the sly his father, back in Troy. Menelaus
                              chuckles. Night falls.
He screws Wifey 6 ways from Sunday as 2 boys under wooly
blankets make explorations, & tender fingers brush *sunrise,
sunrise* across the Spartan sky.

THE SERPENT

KEN POYNER

I try not to be bitter.
I am a thousand generations removed
From the original incident, and anything that has become 'me'
Was not dreamed of in that ancient, self-centered history.
I imagine running,
As though in this generation
I could remember running. Four legs,
And a will to move in the straight,
Not serpentine. Think of it.
My whole life I have wondered
Why Satan would find our form special;
But wondered more why God
Would punish a whole race,
The sons of sons of sons of daughters,
Because some demon with a plan
Thought: why, I'll make myself look
Like that random, unpardonable creature. He
Could have appeared as a bird,
And the birds would be no more at fault
Than were my lightning quick ancestors. But it is not
My damnation to alter. Down here,
Belly to the earth I move

In frightening letters, and calculate
The balance of imagined legs jutting out
Lizard like, the architecture of speed
And of community, of ordinary respect.
I wonder at every retelling whether the story is right:
The man, the woman, the faux serpent,
The taking of what is not one's to take;
Or whether, claiming God's righteous assistance,
And with my curious ancestor balanced vainly on uncaring legs,
Perhaps Satan won the prize he actually wanted.

DEER HUNT

STEPHANIE ALLEN

Driving home from the movie, Luther Carpenter is thinking about the new woman at work. "Madeleine" is her name, "Mad" what she's told everybody in the Bowie Parks and Recreation offices to call her. Since she started a few weeks ago as the new receptionist, he's seen her sashay past the door of his office every day, drawing his attention away from all the budget reports and program proposals he is falling asleep over. Still, he can barely remember Madeleine-call-me-Mad's face. But her ass, well, every man in the office had had his eye on that piece of property since the day she came. This afternoon, for once, Luther had done more than just look.

He'd followed Mad into the west stairwell and found her willing to indulge in a few minutes of all-out groping even sloppier and more delicious than his first attempts in middle school. They'd only stopped when someone opened a door upstairs. He smiles in his car's dark interior, then wipes the expression off his face in case his wife, Evelyn, can see it somehow from the passenger seat. He can't help tapping the index finger of his free hand against the Camry's seat. He's only dimly aware of Evelyn nagging him to slow down when a deer appears out of the darkness, right in the middle of the road ahead of them.

It is the first living thing they have seen on what was supposed to be a shortcut through the Agricultural Research Center, a government facility whose rolling meadows and woods stretch as far and wide as a small town. There had been an accident on U.S. 1, they'd overheard someone say in the crowd leaving the theater after their movie. Snarled traffic, long waits, the prospect of hours wasted on the road. It had been Luther's idea to get home to Laurel by cutting through the research center's deserted grounds and then taking the Baltimore-Washington Parkway north. Twenty minutes, and they would be home from their movie, would be turning down their quiet cul-de-sac, sliding into their cluttered garage, tiptoeing out to the foyer to reset the alarm for the night. That was the plan. And it had still seemed like a good one when they ran across the sawhorses and flashing lights and DETOUR sign routing them off the main road onto the research center's bumpy side roads with names like "Beaver Dam Road" and "Dairy Annex Extension."

Now the deer, risen abruptly in the headlights, just stands there in the middle of the road, carelessly interrupting Luther's daydreams of Madeleine-call-me-Mad, not even bothering to turn its slender head to look at the car hurtling toward it. The animal seems to speed toward them, as if it is gliding sideways up the road somehow. Luther has time to see it, a quick second in which, absurdly enough, the only thought he can snatch from the jumble in his mind is a desire to say to his wife, "Ev, look at that!" But he doesn't say it, or anything else. Before he can react, the deer strikes the car with an enormous, dull *whump!*

The impact jolts them and makes the car shake violently.
The deer slides up the hood of the car, shatters the windshield
and flies off Evelyn's side into the darkness from which it came.
All the while, Luther tries to stop the car, tries to remember
whether he's supposed to pump the brakes or bolt his foot to
the floor and does some of both as he wrestles with the steering
wheel, struggling to keep from running off the road into one of
the trees his panicked mind insists surround them, though his
eyes can make out nothing but a spinning blur.

Finally, the car jerks to a stop. Only then, nose in a ditch
and rear wheels on the shoulder, does Luther actually hear all
the noise: The shrilling of the tires digging for purchase, his
wife screaming, himself screaming, the slash of the car through
underbrush, the crunch of the deer, his heart pounding now so
hard he can't seem to draw a breath for all the hammering.

The windshield is punctured like a ripped fabric in front of
Evelyn. That much Luther can see by moonlight, especially
since the airbags, for some reason, have not deployed. Without
any power in the car, though, he can barely make out Evelyn,
can't even tell whether she is looking through the shattered
window or at him.

An unpleasant warmth spreads through him as he waits for
her to say something about the mess he has gotten them into.
He's sure the car has been seriously damaged. He has no idea
where they are. His wife remains silent, and the seconds
continue to tick by. Until finally Luther senses that this
moment, this random shock, is still molten. That he might
make it into something more for Ev to think about than how

he screwed up on the drive home.

"Stay here," he says, throwing open his door and speaking with an aplomb that surprises him. "I'll go see how bad it is."

The car is worse than he thought. Moonlight shows him a staved-in grille and a bumper popped loose on Evelyn's side. The hood looks like a boulder has dropped on it from out of the sky. The car is dead silent, not even ticking the way it normally does when he kills the ignition after a long ride. Even if he could start it up again, he doubts he'd be able to drive it.

The only damage worse than this that Luther has ever seen up close was to his cousin Mookie's motorcycle when Mookie went skating along a guardrail on Interstate 95 in Connecticut one night long ago, coming home from a pot party. The front wheel was twisted around into a square edge and the whole motor compartment casing was torn away like a wrapper off a candy bar. Mookie kept the damaged bike in the garage for years, liked to show if off and brag about how he just walked away from the wreck. Sometimes, when they were alone, Luther asked his older cousin if they could go out and look at it. Mookie would kid him for a while, then oblige, but Luther was never allowed to stroke the twisted metal.

Standing beside his own damaged vehicle now, he's at a loss as to what he should do. He looks up and down the road, this long, dark snake of a road winding through a cornfield on one side and on the other, an open meadow interrupted by only a few old, big-canopied trees here and there. By day he's seen cows wandering these fields. What he doesn't see, anywhere, is a sign telling him the name of the road, the one that he'll need to give to an emergency dispatcher so help can be sent. Why the hell hadn't he looked where they were going at the last intersection? Evelyn probably had. She missed very few things in this world. He had never told her how he would hate to be one of her students, reading through the comments she put in the margins of his paper about all of the comma splices and dangling modifiers she'd found. Watching her mark up papers in red ink, he sometimes imagined that the point of the pen was a blade and the thin red line that it made was blood seeping from the page.

He glances over his shoulder to see if she is watching him, but he can't see though the dark, shattered windshield, so he turns back, trying to think. That is when he notices there is blood on the grille. It feels warm and sticky on his fingers when he touches it. It is smeared on the white hood, too, like a child's sloppy finger-painting in black. Luther looks into the corn at the roadside, wondering, only now, about the animal that left it there. Where is the deer?

Just off the road, a cornstalk lies bent at a crazy angle, one leaf dabbled with blood. Luther touches that too, unflinchingly, and now he hopes his wife is watching him. Because an idea is forming in his mind, one woven from wisps of adventure movies and threads of cable TV sport shows and vague rituals and stirrings that seem older than his hazy memories of them, somehow. He doesn't stop to try to piece it all together sensibly. His heart, finally slowing to a normal rhythm, takes a last bucking leap in his chest.

"I'm gonna go find it, Ev," he tells her after opening her door a little so she can hear him.

From the dark interior, his invisible wife sighs faintly.

He tries to explain to her, to make sure she'll appreciate the gravity of what he's about to do. "The deer. You can't just, you know, leave it like that if you don't kill it right off, so I guess ... I'll be right back. Yeah."

He doesn't wait to hear what Evelyn will say to this garbled explanation. He's suddenly in a hurry, as if he has been examining the damaged hood for a week now, as if some clock is running down too quickly. He peers at Evelyn once more, searching for the beam of her attention, the focus of her gaze, but it's too dark to see her.

"Stay here," he says, guessing it is the thing to say. He shuts her door and tramps off into the cornfield.

The corn is planted strangely, not the way he thought you were supposed to plant corn. It isn't in rows. On either side of Luther, in the field he's ventured into, it grows, instead, in huge tangled thickets that tower over his head and defy his attempts to peer between the stalks. The floor of the path tunneling between the thickets, he can see dimly, is dried and cracked mud, like the bottom of a river that has risen into the air and baked in the sun.

More like the woods than a cornfield, Luther is thinking about his surroundings, when it occurs to him that he hasn't any weapon to use to finish off the deer. That's what he is going to do, he realizes, though he has never done anything like that before. He could take off his belt and strangle it, though somehow that seems no better than leaving it to bleed to death in the corn somewhere. A solution presents itself almost at once, when a piece of branch crusted with lichen appears on the ground in the middle of his path. The moment he picks it up and hefts it, finds it fits his bloody grasp perfectly, he feels better, feels good. He anticipates the moment when he will tell Evelyn about the death blow, those sad eyes, the snap of his wrist, quick, decisive, accurate. He smiles.

As soon as he sets off again, he hears a moan. Can a deer moan? He didn't think they could, but still he whirls around looking for it, spinning so clumsily he almost falls over. The moan comes again, clearer this time and at the same time more diffuse, as if it is coming from far away and right below him simultaneously. Luther holds the branch out in front of him and parts the nearest corn stalks, but it's no use, he can't see a thing in there without a flashlight. The moon, so bright overhead at the time of the accident, now flickers teasingly as clouds race across its face.

Luther takes a breath and moves down the path, deeper into the corn. The moaning comes more quietly now, but more steadily, something between a sigh, an *ahhhhhh,* and a low hum. It grows neither louder nor softer as he moves along, and it is not long before he begins to feel it inside his clothes, seeping through his skin, moving around like his own thoughts. He takes the branch in both hands and distracts himself with the roughness of the bark, which flakes off as he runs his fingers over it, winnowing it down to wood as hard and smooth as a baseball bat.

The channel between the corn patches bends to the right, dips suddenly, and then straightens again. Well up ahead, Luther can see that it ends at what is probably another road.

He quickens his pace, assuring himself that he is not trying to get away from the moaning, only trying to locate it. The ground moistens, and mud sucks at his shoes. A slight wind rises, confusing the direction of the moaning even further. The moon comes out full again, silvering the corn leaves which, for some reason, are dead here and as dry as the ground is soggy.

He wants to plug his ears against the moaning; instead, he shakes his head to try to clear it. An unwelcome memory assails him. When he was in college, a cat took to crying outside his window at 3 a.m. His ox of a roommate, a guy from Queens named Tony, slept right through it. But Luther couldn't. It would wake him every night and seemingly pin him right to the thin mattress of the upper bunk, helpless to act. Although he knew it was a cat, it had to be, that thin wail, so plaintive, so sad, so insistent, left him weak and panting, and as much as he hated the fact, he could do nothing but listen for weeks until, finally, the cat moved on.

He stops to catch his breath. He hasn't been to the gym in months, and he's feeling it now, now that he could use some endurance. But he has the branch. He fingers the bumps and spikes where smaller twigs have broken off and moves on, swinging the club like a pendulum, letting the motion lull him. *I took care of it,* he hears himself telling his wife when he gets back to the car. *Finished off the damn thing.* He'll snap his fingers, a resounding pop of the knuckles that closes the matter. This doesn't sound quite as merciful as what he'd tried to explain to Evelyn back at the car, but he doesn't bother to amend it.

Instead, he grins a bit. Maybe he'll tell Evelyn the story of how he took care of the deer the next time the two of them get into one of those argument-not-arguments that he hates. One moment they would be just chatting and the next, Evelyn was peppering him with a bunch of questions. Like, "And how long have you been working there, Luther?" and "Don't you think you deserve a raise?" and "Will not discussing it make it any better?" Evelyn, patient like she's talking to an idiot, never accusing, never raising her voice, just doing that flicking thing with her fingers like she's got a cigarette, though she doesn't smoke and never has. They'd been having one of these argument-not-arguments when he collided with the deer.

Ooooohhhhhh. More voice than breath now, the moaning rises again, almost a word. Luther's skin congeals at the sound of it, tightens across his arms and his neck and his chest, the tightness traveling down him in a wave. He wants to be done with this. Where the hell is the deer? He hasn't seen a single dent in the wall of corn where it might have gone crashing into the stalks as a wounded animal should, moving in a blood-sapped delirium, blind, stupid, easy to find. He hasn't seen any more droplets of blood or smears of it on the leaves, either. And shouldn't he have seen hoof prints in the soft mud? There are none in front of him. He turns around and looks behind himself. All he sees are his own zigzagging shoeprints. Evelyn is probably wondering what is taking him so long. He pushes the thought out of his mind.

Then the moaning grows fainter, fainter but continuous, so that he can hardly distinguish it from the whispering wind moving through the cornstalks and the buzzing it has set up in his head, rising and falling in time, refusing his attempts to snuff it out. His breath comes even more heavily now. He breaks into a staggering run he can barely sustain for all the slipping his shoes do in the muddy ground, but he keeps it up anyway, straining for the road ahead, for the pavement he can now see in the moonlight. *One blow. One blow.* Just before Luther reaches the road, something grabs his feet. He flies for an instant and then slams face-first into cool, rock-hard blacktop.

For some time, he can't move. The impact echoes just like the impact of the deer did, visiting upon him as he lies helpless the sounds of the grinding of his own skull against the road and the *whoosh* of air punched from his chest. When he can finally draw a full breath, his pains announce themselves. His raw palms bubble with invisible fire that spreads to his knees, bloody through his torn pants when he sits up. His bones feel intact but altered, as if they might now shatter and slice through his flesh if he so much as sneezes. He touches his forehead and finds the abrasion there sticky with blood and debris. The road and stalks and night sky around him lurch and waver, letting him know that walking upright will be treacherous. He wonders whether this is even a little of how the deer felt when he plowed his Toyota into its side.

He waves that thought away. Then he waves a few more times before he realizes there are flies pestering him. They drone around his head, looping in persistent circles until he turns himself around, and as soon as he does he sees in the darkness the shadowy form of what tripped him. The carcass of the deer lies in perfect stillness on the shoulder of the road, its legs a tangle, its torso a curving mound, its head hidden by the bulk of its body.

It's dead! He's sure of it. A flicker of elation riffles through him; he is done, *done*, and he can go back to the car and get the hell out of this maze of roads and corn and shadows and lunatic noises. If Evelyn asks about it, he'll just make something up. Luther tries to fabricate a few details, but he finds himself swatting at flies that become so numerous that they make him forget his half-baked story and climb stiffly to his feet. Standing unsteadily, he can see the deer's head. The head is antlered, crowned by branches and points like a winter tree.

Not the same deer. The one he hit had been much smaller and bareheaded, a female. A doe.

A torrent of flies comes pouring out of a gaping, black maw where the buck's belly should be, and a stench he somehow hadn't noticed before makes Luther fasten his arm over his mouth and nose. Gagging, his eyes watering, he stumbles backward into the middle of the road and vomits.

When he's done, he wipes his mouth on his sleeve slowly, trying to regain his composure. *Get a hold of yourself,* he tells himself. *It's just a dead deer.* He's seen plenty of the damn things on the side of the road, thrown there when they were hit by cars like his own. A wave of nausea sweeps over him again. Clutching his stomach, he turns a slow circle, looking for his car, its familiarity, its shelter and Ev there waiting for him for what, five, ten, maybe fifteen minutes now? Where he's left her all alone. Did he do that? Just walk off and leave his wife by herself in the dark in the middle of nowhere? She hadn't said a word to stop him, either. He shakes his head, which makes him dizzy again, forcing him to bend over and plant his hands on his knees to steady himself. What is he supposed to do now?

Then Luther Carpenter laughs at himself and says, "Shit!" out loud in the night and the sound of his own voice, normal and solid, steadies him. He stands up. He *does* have a story to tell. Not to Evelyn, but to the fellas at the game next Sunday. Yeah. *Out there wandering around in a cornfield like some got-damn hick,* he'll say, and he'll effect a bucktoothed, hayseed grin that will crack everybody up. *The damn thing was stone-cold dead before I could even fuck it up for wrecking my car! You believe that shit?* Finally he's got a tale to throw out there, like they've been prodding him for, one to top even *their* bullshit. He's almost overcome with giggles just thinking about it.

Feeling restored, he sets off down the road, intending to keep turning right at every junction until he's circled back around to the car. Simple. It might take ten minutes, maybe fifteen, depending on how big the patch of corn is. The night is silent around him. The moaning or whatever it was has stopped. There's not even the rustle of a breeze.

Not far along, the pavement ends abruptly under his feet. Luther halts, as if he has inadvertently stepped off a cliff and has an instant to fling himself back, cartoon-like. Who would just stop paving a road? What kind of people did shit like that? He stands there a moment, toeing the loose dirt and pebbles, imagining himself putting it into just those words for his buds Stu and Maytag. That gets him walking again, walking and grinning, thinking about watching the game with his dawgs on Sunday, telling his story at halftime after they've all had a few, everybody cracking up. And later, the inevitable moment when Maytag chides Luther about his life. "Shit like that wouldn't be happening to you, man, if you just get the *fuck* out of the burbs and c'mon back *home*. You hear me? Back to the city where shit is *real*." Maytag always manages to adapt his ribbing about the suburbs to the details at hand, though it dawns on Luther, as he trudges along, that one thing stays the same: the invitation to come back to the fold never extends to Evelyn.

Then a thought strikes Luther, the best idea he's had all night. Why wait? Maytag and Stu, they'd drive up here and get him if he called them. He wouldn't have to rely on some greasy vulture in a tow truck who'd charge double just because he had Luther by the balls. Luther grabs for his phone, anticipating Maytag's rasping voice, but the pocket where it should be is empty. His wallet is missing, too. The only item that's where it belongs is his keychain, full of useless keys.

He looks behind himself, back down the road, to gauge how far he's come since falling on his face. He can't see the carcass from here, but he knows he doesn't want to go near it again, to crawl around beside it looking for his things. He stands there empty-handed and a bit disoriented at the thought of his credit cards and IDs and driver's license all scattered over the road back there. And his phone, the black pane where he's grown accustomed to seeing the broken and bug-eyed reflection of himself, its screen now full of clouds.

As Luther stands staring, something lopes across the road, moving fluidly, like a bird shadow flows over the ground. In the wan light of the shrouded moon, it is impossible to tell what it was. After a few seconds, Luther wonders whether he really saw anything at all. Then it ripples back across the road again, a little closer this time, a dark and slippery oval without visible legs that vanishes into the wall of corn.

Could it be the deer? After all this time? Luther stares at the spot where it crossed, as if that will tell him how the wounded doe could possibly have gotten behind him. "It's confused and, and running in circles," he stammers out loud. There. And how could it be moving so fast, so easily, after being struck by a car? That one takes him a several uneasy moments. "It's a different deer, that's how. Another one. This place is crawling with them."

And why would a deer be following him instead of running away?

Luther turns around and walks briskly, refusing to slow down as his knees begin to protest and a banging starts up in his head. If he just keeps turning left—no, *right, right*—if he just keeps turning right, it has to take him back to the car. He glances behind himself and sees nothing. That doesn't reassure him in the least. He hurries a little faster.

The next time he turns for a look behind him, the cornstalks ten feet back are waving and bending, and dried husks and withered ears of corn go scattering into the road. *There's nothing there,* Luther tells himself, but he walks faster, nearly a jog now. His breath starts to skip and stutter. A flash-fire panic shoots through his innards. Battered and bruised and woozy as he is, his body still tenses up with adrenaline, ready to flee, as the shimmering sweeps toward him.

But flee where? Whatever this is, he has walked right into it, hasn't he? Went seeking it, in fact, didn't he? The voice in his head asking him nasty questions is not Ev's anymore, it's his own. Ev's questioning, that argument-not-an-argument they'd been having in the car, was different, wasn't it? He had been telling her about a new project at Parks and Rec that would be keeping him late at work, an ad campaign built around the phrase "Get off your butt and exercise!" It sounded so good as he was spinning it out in the car that he didn't pay much attention to the details he was making up. When he finally fell silent, Ev had said nothing for a long time. Then, "So you're looking forward to this?" He assured her he was, despite all the work. "Was it your idea?" she asked, almost inaudible. For some reason, he only nodded. "I guess I should have expected it, shouldn't I?"

They'd hit the deer before he could answer.

Luther comes to a halt. It had been no argument.

Around him, the commotion in the corn moves forward, beyond him, up the road across an intersection and a little beyond before it dissipates. The corn settles back to stillness. Luther looks around. The calmed September air hangs cool and dark around him. To his left, the road stretches onward into darkness. To his right, twenty feet away, a white car sits on the shoulder.

His and Ev's Camry. Now he sees her as he must have left her after the deer nearly broke through the windshield in front of her, after the impact threw her left and right before the car skidded to a jolting stop. Her face sliced by the glass blown into the car's interior by the body of the doe. The blue-black bruises across her ribs from the seatbelt, the obscene swelling of the arm she threw out to protect herself, broken against the Camry's door.

This time, when he runs, he feels not awkward but slow. He

calls out to her the whole time, though she probably can't hear him, though there's not much point. Finally, Luther reaches the car. When he pulls the handle of Ev's door, the interior of the Camry is empty.

Confused, he looks across the hood. The damage from the impact remains, the smears of blood now dry. He steps in front of the car and looks around. Ten feet beyond the car, Evelyn is there, standing on the shoulder, the pale fabric of her dress fluttering around her calves. For some moments, he can do nothing more than stare at her to convince himself that she is really there.

When he reaches her, he gathers her into his arms, and the heat of her skin, the faint, coconut scent of her hair oil, finally convince him. She remains stiff. When he lets her go and takes a step backward, she doesn't even look at him. In the moonlight, he follows her gaze.

The doe lies just off the shoulder of the road, panting and twitching weakly.

"I called Animal Control," Evelyn says hoarsely. Then she looks at him, her dark eyes large and motionless. "All I got was a recording."

On the ground, a few feet away, the doe writhes like she is trying to get to her feet and then collapses again. Blood covers her body and throat, and blood drips from her mouth as well. Clutched in Evelyn's arms is a rock the size of a pot roast.

Luther considers what is in front of him. He takes the rock from Evelyn, who offers no resistance. The weight of it is surprising, greater than he thought, but it is no strain to hold it in one hand as he thinks. He feels a calm now, a calm that suffuses him without him calling for it. The doe at his feet gasps a bloody snort and he kneels, coming down close to her head. One dark eye rolls toward him and then the doe jolts and gasps, contorting again. Luther sits the rock on the ground, lets it roll away down the embankment. He sighs, leans forward. He cradles the large, awkward head in his arms, lowers the register of his voice, relaxes his sound, speaks to her: *All right, now,* he says. *All right.*

MISS TUDOR, CORNTOWN MIDDLE SCHOOL, THE ALL-VOLUNTEER ARMY

WILLIAM JOLLIFF

Miss Tudor was the captain of her class.
Her fierce insinuations kept her rank—
such contempt for sloppy cursive, mumbled words,
for fools, *small fools,* who fail to carry the three.

The farm boys didn't mind their knuckles rapped
but it was hard to untangle the shame,
so at noon they'd head out to the football field
to trade their anger for some good clean pain.

By sixteen they were primed to leave town,
but, with Goodyear and Whirlpool laying off
or closing down, there weren't many places
to go. And there were always recruiters around.

Must I assume, then, that none, none of you recall
that Afghanistan is north, north of Pakistan?
Most of them know that now, Miss Tudor,
though they may not come home to tell you.

BREAKDOWN IN DALLAS

Ryan Ridge

See Coach screaming his head off into his headset on the opposing sideline down in Dallas, dry-erase clipboard in one hand, doublewide water bottle cocktail in the other.

Coach!

He looks like a professional poker player fresh from a Vegas championship. He's wearing his trademark, black Wayfarer sunglasses and a white plastic-visor despite the fact that tonight's game is in a dome in Dallas.

Coach!

He's rail-thin and balding and with what's left he's gone gray, and sure, these days he's seen better, but haven't we all?

Coach!

Like so many Americans he feels foreign to himself. Still, Coach coaches despite it and through it. It's why they call him Coach, at least for now.

Coach!

Among players, past and present, Coach commands respect.

Amongst other career football coaches, Coach is considered a coach's coach, the best kind of coach. He's known for his witty aphorisms on Twitter. They call Coach's Twitter aphorisms

Coachisms. Here are a few:

- Success is nothing less than the cessation of failure.
- Tomorrow is yesterday the day after tomorrow.
- Never mistake mistakes for mistakes. Sometimes they're just opportunities in a different disguise.
- I urge reporters to report better.

With regard to the sporting press, Coach is both reviled and revered.

Between bartenders, Coach is known as a real cool customer with a lava hot wallet.

Because lately Coach drinks.

Because lately Coach drinks a lot.

Because lately, because, because…

Coach drinks a lot lately to surpass the sorrows of this world, the imminent divorce proceedings and the high-profile pressure of his professional life. He boozes before and after practice, at work, and during games. However, he drinks responsibly, he thinks, at work, during games, especially in marquee matchups like tonight's contest against the wild card contending Cowboys, and Coach knows that the outcome of this game will certainly decide two things: 1.) The opponent's playoff hopes, and 2.) Coach's job prospects, namely the future of his future with this team or any other franchise for that matter, and so now Coach is numbing out a bit, cooling off from this fiery planet on this nervous night in Dallas, and he's cutting straight through the stress with a double-wide water bottle filled with fruit punch Gatorade spiked with vodka, Southern Comfort, grenadine, and two twists of lime. He had the water boy mix him up a real stiff one in the locker room at the half. A Hillbilly Hurricane is what Coach calls this concoction. Category None, baby!

Oh, that's perfection, Coach says to the water boy after squeezing out a sip on the sideline as the second half kickoff kicks off.

My pleasure, Coach, the water boy says. I've been practicing at home.

Then the water boy waits an extra beat, doesn't leave, and so Coach tugs a twenty from his fat clip of cash, hands him the bill, and says: For your efforts, Bobby. This a fine drink right here. Be proud. You put your all into it and did you remember the grenadine? If so, that's an extra point.

Yessir.

Atta boy.

He hands Bobby another twenty.

See that golf cart over yonder beyond the end zone?

The one at the paramedic's station?

Yes, Coach says, I want you to go and get it.

You want me to steal it?

Steal is perhaps too strong of a verb, Bobby boy. No, I'd like you to go and play nice and borrow it.

Why, Coach?

Because I want to ride that thing out of here after we storm back victorious and win this game. I think it's the proper thing to do. End this miserable season with some panache.

Why, Coach?

Don't ask why, son. That's an epistemological question and we don't have time for philosophy tonight. Why football? Why

Sunday? Why anything? The answer is: I don't know. Why not?

Coach doesn't know.

Coach doesn't know what he doesn't know.

Coach could write an autobiography about all the things he doesn't know as of late, call it: *Blindsided & Sideways: a Memoir of My Losing Season.*

Coach thinks it'd sell a bazillion copies. Folks like reading about famous losers' lives because it makes them feel better about their own lives of quiet desperation, he thinks.

But now Coach thinks he'd rather not think. He'd rather not think because he knows that even with a Super Bowl ring on his finger and dual division championships under his belt that this imperfect season is going to cost him. It's already cost him his wife, Diana, spouse of twenty-seven years, and sure, maybe their lover's knot had been scissored by the sharp progress of time for some time now, but Coach chalks up this forsaken season as the final frayed edge of a marriage, or the end of the "mirage" as Coach pronounces it these days. Aside from his marriage, this season also cost Coach a small fortune in Cleveland: a $50,000 fine for referring to a few AP reporters as a "flock of cocksuckers" in a post-game press conference, and tonight, down on the opposing sideline in Dallas, facing a huge second half deficit, Coach figures the outcome of this game will cost him the rest. It'll cost him his job. It'll cost him his pride. At least what's left of what's left of it.

Now it's late in the third quarter and Bobby the water boy has returned with the mini-ambulance and plied Coach with another doublewide water bottle cocktail and Coach's players are on the field playing, but they're hardly playing, and Coach can tell that these dudes aren't having any fun—and what's the use of playing if you're not having any fun? Paycheck, is Coach's guess. And save for Bobby's inspirational pours it's been a real uninspired effort all around tonight and speaking of, Coach can't fathom the last time he felt that old thrilling feeling of advancement, achievement, of winning. Despite his current buzz, Coach feels and has felt stagnant and stuck for some time. Maybe, Coach thinks, I should turn it all over to a higher power, sober up, buckle down, and find Jesus. I don't know.

He doesn't know.

Coach doesn't even know where to begin to find Jesus. He looks to the end zone and admires the cheerleaders' legs. He's always had a thing for cheerleaders and legs. Sure, he's knows it's a cliché, or possibly it's a fetish, and Coach also knows that he shouldn't objectify anyone but he can't help himself. Coach likes cheerleaders and legs and he doesn't know why. Others folks like guns or drugs or real estate and he doesn't know why.

Coach likes what he likes and doesn't know why.

Coach feels sad suddenly and doesn't know why.

Coach!

Coach looks up from the sideline and now he sees something shameful emerge on to the Jumbotron. He sees the score of tonight's inevitable blowout loss: 31-3—sure, he knew that at halftime, the score hasn't changed since—but as his eyes scroll across the enormous console he sees a face that's both familiar and strange. On the massive screen Coach sees the face of utter desperation. He lifts his sunglasses and sees his own face, large and luminous on the screen.

And that's enough for Coach. His team is getting trounced and it's the last game of the season besides and Coach is beside himself because they're not going to win a single goddamn game this season and it may be Coach's last game period is the rumor in the press and on the blogs and so Coach figures since he's halfway smashed and totally screwed he might as well take some chances, have some fun; make some memories. Go out big. Do it in style.

His hands are shaking. He's breathing heavy.

Are you all right, Coach? asks Bobby.

Hand me that bucket, please, son, he says.

This one? Bobby asks.

Is there another one?

Bobby hands Coach the big orange Gatorade bucket and Coach hands Bobby another twenty.

Careful, it's heavy, Bobby says.

Things are about to get heavy, says Coach.

What?

Get that getaway car ready.

Huh?

Wait for my cue.

Okay.

So, just before the third quarter comes to a close, Coach trots on out to the fifty-yard line in between downs down in Dallas and he stands in the center of the giant blue star at the center of the field and he's standing there bear-hugging the orange bucket filled with ice and fruit punch Gatorade and as he lifts the container the television cameras zoom in on him and now Coach is 71 feet tall and 180 feet wide on the

Jumbotron and all around him all the players have taken off their helmets and they're mostly scratching their heads and wondering what the hell is happening and then what Coach does is he removes the lid from the bucket, and he hoists it skyward, and just before Coach sacrifices his career and credibility on live television, he pauses, breathes, contemplates life, considers his wife, wonders if she's at home watching this on their big flatscreen in Fort Lauderdale... His daughter at art school in Savannah... His old man in Nashville... His mother in the next world... Coach decides it doesn't matter if they're watching. He's doing it. Yes, he's making a huge mistake right now and he knows it, but he does it anyway. Why not? Sometimes mistakes aren't mistakes, but rather opportunities in a different disguise. He wrote that, once, on Twitter and it went viral.

So he turns the Gatorade bucket over slow and dumps the contents onto his head on live TV. It's a dramatic scene, this scene, and Coach says: So long, suckers. I quit. Sometimes you have to quit to win, Coach thinks, and as the Gatorade stains Coach's white polo shirt red, time slows down, and he looks around at everyone looking at him: the players, the fans, cheerleaders, camera crews, referees, etc.—and now he feels like some madman gladiator of Roman times somehow standing at the postmodern epicenter of a football field in Dallas, Texas, below a colossal Jumbotron, with both middle fingers extended on national television.

He throws in the towel, and when Coach throws in the towel he literally throws in the towel, meaning he removes his sweat-soaked sweat towel from his back pocket and tosses it at a nearby referee.

Provoked, the ref steps back—shocked—and reaches down and picks up the towel. Then he flicks Coach in the face with it.

Coach confiscates the towel and then he smacks the ref in the face with it and that's enough. The ref drops a yellow flag and kicks Coach out of the game.

The announcers are perplexed by these developments. The color guy says he's never seen anything like it. He calls it a complete demonstration of total insanity. In fact, the color guy says, it appears that Coach has lost his mind. He may need help, serious. I'm worried about him, concerned.

The other analyst agrees, says that Coach's antics defy analysis. What is Coach doing? he asks.

The answer is he's lying down on the stretcher in the mini-ambulance on the sideline. Bobby's by his side in the driver's seat saying: What now?

Drive, says Coach. Fast!

Coach!

So long, Coach.

Farewell, Coach. Goodbye.

Coach is Coach and Coach is gone.

Thrown out.

Ejected.

Sure, he gets ejected but not entirely dejected.

The television cameras track his movements on the sidelines and Coach is really moving in that mini-ambulance. He's sitting shotgun in the stretcher seat and Bobby's speeding away. Coach is saying, Faster, son. Get me out of here.

I'm trying, Coach. This is as fast as it goes. Hey, Coach?

What, Bobby?

Are you all right?

I don't know, Coach says. I don't know.

Coach doesn't know.

Coach doesn't know what he doesn't know.

He can't tell if he's cracking up or breaking down or both.

If Coach were to write book about the things he doesn't know, he'd call this unfortunate chapter either *Crackup in Texas* or *Breakdown in Dallas*.

But for now he's on a golf cart, splayed out on a stretcher next to his accomplice, Bobby, the water boy, who's helping Coach make his escape, and now they're at the twenty-yard line and headed toward the tunnel to the locker room but first they make a quick pit stop in the Cowboy's end zone, and then Coach sits up and starts hitting on a squadron of hometown cheerleaders. He can't help it. If it weren't for what's between his own legs he'd be short on brains.

Now Coach hones in on one cheerleader in particular. She's a bombshell, brunette with legs that go up, up, up like skyscraper elevators. Coach says: Why don't you come back to the hotel with me and tomorrow we'll wake up on the right side of history.

And amazingly, somehow, his proposition works, because as soon as Coach makes his pass she drops her pompoms and hops onto the back of the golf cart.

Still got it, Coach thinks, feeling good, as Bobby steers them toward the tunnel and into the locker room. What Coach doesn't know yet is that the cheerleader is in the middle of her own existential crises. What Coach doesn't know is that cheerleaders can't earn a living cheering. What Coach doesn't know now is the location of his sports coat.

Bobby, where's my goddam jacket?

Right here, Coach.

Meanwhile, back inside the stadium, the crowd goes wild, wilder than wild.

Because everyone appreciates a good spectacle within a spectacle, and everyone admires these games within the game.

Coach is Coach and Coach is gone.

Thanks, Coach! Thanks for the memories.

Coach!

Back on the field, the play continues without Coach.

He's later seen on the Jumbotron, wearing sunglasses and a sharkskin suit, leaving the premises in a convertible limousine with a cheerleader in tow.

It's the beginning of the fourth quarter. Sunday evening. Week 16. One team without a coach. One coach without a team.

There he goes.

There goes Coach in a convertible limousine with the top down on an unseasonably warm night in Dallas, riding off into the early-December sunset with a mysterious woman by his side. My life is so terrible and beautiful I could cry, thinks Coach.

And he does.

WORKING MIDNIGHTS

Janet Hagelgans

It's his broken body clock that wakes him up at 9 A.M.
Sitting on the living room sofa still in uniform. Gun belt
and everything. A crick in his neck from sleeping

in his Kevlar. Strange to wake up dressed for killing
surrounded by couch cushions and carvings of ducks.
Peaches spoiling on the counter. Strange it's just as

quiet here as it was out there when it snowed
through his whole shift. He drove around the town
alone in no particular pattern. Watched the large flakes fall.

CONCEALED CARRY

PETER MAKUCK

Admit it or not,
we're all packing
 a cold weight
close to the heart,
tapping the ribs,
but so well hidden
 we pass unnoticed
by friends, colleagues,
and guards,
 never trip an alarm
and we're not sure why.

Things that happened,
 years ago
or just now—
things begging
for apology or payback—
that look of disgust,
those spat-out words
 or worse.

So we carry,
always helpless
before those smirky looks,
before the loud pop
          and spatter,
the slump and collapse,

before they rise
          like the undead
with the same look
that makes us
reach for another clip,
firing again
     and again
          and again

GOLDEN HORIZONS
Emily Koon

I don't have the heart to tell Donald, that mauve tracksuit he wears makes his behind look like two hams stuffed in a sack.

Every morning, he visits me here at the old people prison, then goes to ride the elliptical at the Young Men's Christian Association. Always wearing that tracksuit, I don't even have the heart to tell him. Before he leaves, he kisses me on my forehead and says not to pull my hair out. I guess he doesn't want a baldheaded woman.

Donald is good to me. I wrote it in shaving cream on the bathroom mirror to remind me. When he asks what it means, I say the cleaning woman must have done it, that her husband's name must be Donald, too. The words are all stickyfuzzylike on the glass, the cream a week dried, but I won't let anybody wipe it off.

"Eva, come on," Donald says. He says that a lot. *Come on, let's get in the car. Come on, get out of the tub, your fingers are prunes.* He's good to me. I know because I wrote it on the mirror.

"For better or worse," I say. I want to sound like I got a few of my marbles left, even if I don't.

He doesn't smile or say anything because he's looking for

new cracks in me. Before he got me a room here, he would talk to my sister on the phone about how big the old cracks had got. Deep, like somebody took an axe and split my soul.

He said he was too old for this. I am fifty-eight, and Donald is older than that.

He loves me even though I'm a pain in the ass, is how he'll tell you things are between us, is what he says as he's leaving for the day. It fixes things for a while, but he still watches for new cracks. He watches to see what comes out of the old ones.

Suzanne the administrator woman who I call The Warden says today is my anniversary here at Golden Horizons. One year since Donald brought me in and said *Well, isn't this nice? They got rocking chairs and everything.*

A few months before that, I walked off from the psychiatrist's while Donald was in Walgreens. He must have got restless waiting for my appointment to let out, no TV or anything to look at, so he went across the street for a Coca Cola and some peanuts to put in the bottle. Before he knew it, he'd sat down at the little machine where you check your blood pressure with the cuff pulled tight as it would go. He felt his blood pumping hard. It felt so good he did it twice, *proof of a beating heart,* he said, *proof positive of aliveness.* He was thinking of doing it again when he noticed the time.

It was just a minute or two he missed me by; if he'd run, he'd have seen me turning the corner onto Elm Street. (On account of plantar warts, Donald will only run if his life depends on it.)

Two hours later, he found me at Henny Penny's, skinning

drumsticks. The skins made a greasy pile on the tray as I pulled the meat off the bones and ate it with my fingers. While I finished, Donald sat there sipping his Coke with the peanuts floating it, studying on what to do. I offered but he didn't want any of the skins. He must have thought they looked like the remains of people whose souls had left them.

Before the chicken place, I sat in the sanctuary at the Methodist church waiting for Jesus who never showed up. Before the church, I went into the Wells Fargo skyscraper and took out chicken money.

Way before any of that, I'm talking years, I drove through the Piggly Wiggly cashier, who'd run out after me waving my receipt. At the time I thought she had a terrible reason for running out, some news I wasn't going to like. Someone I loved dead, my credit card stolen to buy filthy magazines. I drove clean through her so as not to find out what. She came apart so easy, like she was made of smoke, like she was already a ghost to start with.

My sister Sherry was next to me in the front seat. Her face is completely different now, but back then she had the same face as me. She has one of those celebrity button noses now that nobody's ever born with. She'll tell you it changed her whole life. It changed her whole face, anyway.

She pressed her foot into an imaginary brake pedal but couldn't stop us crashing through that poor woman.

The chicken place was some kind of last straw. After that, Sherry's second husband the schoolteacher told Donald I should be put somewhere. *A place where she can be cared for properly. Someplace compassionate, of course.* I reckon it wasn't fair, having to see me at all the functions. Our whole lives until Sherry got her new nose, people mixed up our faces. That wasn't fair either. It's why she spent that year living in a box and our parents and even occasionally Donald went on Saturdays and talked to her through the glass, which was a box within a box. The box was full of women whose faces got mixed up with other people's, so I don't think she was ever lonely.

"How about that, Mrs. Tucker?" The Warden smiles her big white teeth at me, a you've just won the *Publishers Clearing House Sweepstakes* smile. I pretend I don't hear and sort of don't because I'm worried about how I'm going to get into the front garden.

"You know you can't go out there right now, Mrs. T. It isn't time for Horticultural Therapy," The Warden says. She holds out a stationery set with my name on it in stupid-looking calligraphy script. *From the Desk of Mrs. Eva Tucker,* my prize for getting locked up in here.

"Why don't you go sit on your big behind and let other people live?" I say. I push down on the door's metal bar, but nothing happens. I'm trapped here, me and these brainrotted old people not knowing their own children. Some of them carry their feces around. They bring it to meals and talk to it like it's a baby. You have to be careful what you take out of their hands.

"I don't even have a desk in my room," I mumble at the glass door. I'm talking to a woman named Helen I used to know, who got me to shave my head that one time. If I'm on the drugs they give me here, I know she wasn't a real person, just a thing I made up out of loneliness, but I talk to her anyway.

As the two motorcycles roar into the front circle, Ralph Davenport is stuck in one of his time loops. John Fitzgerald Kennedy's death is just a couple years old, the brains and hunks of skull all over that pretty woman still a horror to people. Somebody knows something. He goes on about Jack Ruby and the Warren Commission until I want to shove the papers from my stationery set in his mouth.

Both machines are shiny and black, and Ruby was dying of cancer; somebody had to know that.

"That's my husband," I say, half to Helen and half to Ralph Davenport, before Donald even takes his helmet off.

People like that never act alone.

I tell Ralph Davenport to be quiet, but he keeps trying to work it out, why a person would do a thing like that.

"You got to let me wipe that mirror down, Mrs. T. Suzanne's gonna do an inspection and can my ass," says the cleaning woman, whose name is Roberta.

I don't care for language like that, but Roberta is all right. She has calluses on the inside. She's raising her grandchild alone, a person not put off by other people's fluids and grime. These are things I can respect. When she finds my pills in the trash she doesn't say anything; she sticks them in a little pocket in her pinafore.

I don't want her to get in trouble, so I let her in. After she wipes the mirror down with something that smells like melted rubber, I forget what I'm supposed to remember about Donald.

I know his friend is waiting in the lobby because of the slow way the staff women shake their heads when he walks in. They can smell the indecency. Last time she stayed outside on her bike. She took her helmet off, and I saw she had straight steel-colored hair pulled into silver ponytail tube down her back. A divorcee, maybe one of those women's libbers that never got married.

"The kind of person who says things like *life starts at fifty*," I tell Helen, who I know would have agreed.

Donald says he hasn't done anything he's ashamed of. He talks about companionship and platonic love between men and women. He's not wearing that mauve track suit but a new pair of Wrangler blue jeans that are a little highwater on him. I tell him how his butt looks. When he goes in the bathroom to look, he sees the history of our lives written in shaving cream loops on the mirror. It's soft and powdery smelling and still wet, something that would feel good, sliding into a pool of it. When he comes out, I have to hold him in my arms for a long time while he weeps.

INSOMNIAC
Matt Morgan

If death is a sort of sleep, I will never die.
Your heirlooms will disappear; your watchdog
will dream through the raptured night,
and I will never die.

This is how I sleep: awake
in darkness, searching out over cool asphalt,
slipping past your bolted locks.
If you had the time, I might show you
where everything goes. How there is a great warehouse
harbored out of the way, like an isle of lepers.

Here I might pull your childhood Lovie off a shelf,
and you might hold it again, cradle the spit-crusted
doll against your breast

and rock yourself back into an older carth.
There is no harm in pretending, you might say,
no harm in any of this at all—

and you would be wrong.

A single leaf clings to your moon-blue window
as if encased in the glass itself. It intrudes
seamlessly into my own passing reflection.

If you haven't noticed, I've found a way
of walking inside these unlocked hours
without casting even a shadow of truth.

There is no squeak in the floorboard
I can't tip-toe around. There is no other life
to wake up to. No other future to find.

There is only the sudden draft in the room—
the sweat-soaked sheets clinging to your skin—
the cataplectic night stretching back your eyes.

THE SORROW TREE
David White

The summer is its own Susanna
and cataracts a panorama of early sorrow.

The arbor growing wild outside the window,
the arbor, silent, amnesic deletory of the day,

Sways shushed patterns of sound and sight
to the tune of the morning traffic.

Distantly, as breath of cooling earth,
you could not heed our bereavement,

you could not heed bereavement,
could not see with eyes, and without eyes

peek into our windows, peek into
our cupboards, into our drawers,

shed your male-sex sperls,
touch with handless bark

the walls, the verbena, the lobelia
touch with bark the thyme.

You peek and poke, you peek
and consider with clematis-thoughts

consider in ways that baffle.
I'd reject my skin in a moment

to consider what you consider
between the apartment walls

beneath your hair of air.

IRIS

Connie Green

Quaker Lady, the garden book names
this shade—pale lavender verging
on the beige of spring oaks, color

seeping petal to petal, frizz of beard
like fluff of cattails too long in the sear
of sun. I have come to cut stems

for my mother, her brain cells
like the iris rhizomes, tangled and twisted,
their flowering a stubborn stand born

of black earth and granite will, of flex
and force, sap spiraling into blade,
spines erect this spring morning

while earth lurches from equinox
to solstice, and Quaker Ladies mass
among mossy stones of an old wall.

A TIME BEFORE
KATRINA NORFLEET

The river that was once my backyard calls me to it. It's a hushed whisper that replays like a refrain until it lulls me like a church hymn and beckons me to follow its hum. So I drive the rented minivan onto the long stretch of highway marked by a red, white, and blue 95 North sign heading to my hometown. Headed to Haverstraw, where the Hudson waits for me—a place to lay my burdens down.

We watched as two mules pulled the rickety wooden wagon through the streets of Atlanta that April afternoon in 1968. Dr. Martin Luther King, Jr.'s mahogany casket lay inside. The streets were filled with the one-hundred-thousand-plus mourners because Ebenezer Baptist church couldn't hold them. The events played out on the screen in a box within a box with the all-white news team commentating moment by moment. That's when Big Ma started to call on Jesus. It's when she just couldn't take anymore, and she shut out the rest of the broadcast coming from the console that sat in the corner of our front room.

Her spirit was heavy, strained by what may only be explained as a sensing that death was on its way to visit her, too. So she left the room hoping to ward off any likeness to the widow veiled in black who courageously led the funeral procession for her dead husband.

But the news came anyway, on the very next day. I watched through a vent—a black grate placed on the ceiling above the gas heater in the kitchen. From the second story floor I saw Big Ma carry on below like some of the women did on Sundays when the Holy Ghost got a hold of them. She shouted and she shouted. Then she cried out, "Sweet Jesus!" before she lost her balance and fell back onto the pew disguised as a well-worn cloth rocking chair.

That evening, our house filled with people. Family and church folks in shades of brown bearing gifts secured in aluminum foil and plastic wrap: southern-style fried chicken, rice pudding, pound cake made without a boxed recipe, and bowls of potatoes and boiled eggs cut into pieces, mixed together with Hellman's mayonnaise, Gulden's mustard, pickled relishes and topped with paprika.

Buicks, Chevys, Pontiacs, and Fords lined West Street as their owners paid their respects to our family.

Pop was gone. He passed away. He's in heaven now.

That's what they told me.

It's August of 2005 and I'm traveling back to Haverstraw with my sister riding shotgun and our mother and children in the backseats of the rented vehicle. Eleven months have passed since my husband called me on the telephone and said, "I'm not coming back home. I'm not happy."

Pulling off New York's Palisades Parkway and onto the familiar roads that lead to the town where I grew up brings into view the postcard-worthy landscape of mountains to the right and the expansive Hudson River to the left. Less than twelve hours before, after another bruising conversation with my estranged husband, I sat in my own car in the parking lot outside my neighborhood's twenty-four-hour CVS Pharmacy in a Maryland suburb outside of Washington D.C. In the front seat of the Toyota Camry, I had a little talk with Jesus that ended my three-year plea to heal our marriage. I had what my sister would describe as a Rosa Parks moment. I was tired. Good and tired. Plenty tired. Tired enough to confess to God for the first time, "I don't want to do this anymore."

But now, with the gentle flowing river in sight, the tension leaves and the comfort sets in. Something akin to nostalgia rubs up against me and tries to become my new best friend. It's a yearning for something I can't name. Yet I hear its call, a bittersweet welcome back to a place I still call home after moving away some twenty-five years ago.

We, the six of us, were supposed to be at Virginia Beach for the week, but a timeshare mix-up left us scrambling to find a way to keep a promise to three middle schoolers longing for a summer vacation where exams and homework were as distant as a third cousin, twice removed. They weren't alone. I ached for space far away from our house, where the walls were now splattered with melancholy—the handiwork of a moved-out husband and part-time dad. Endless visions of sweet, breezy ocean-side evenings paired with a beach chair and paperback book had been the balm on my open wound.

But our best laid plans to vacation at an oceanfront condo have transitioned into a six-night stay at my brother's house located in the village of Haverstraw.

The day of Pop's funeral, I rode to Fairmount Baptist Church in the black limousine owned by George M. Holt Funeral Home. Mr. Holt was a white man but he did all the colored people's undertakings. I sat on the front pew next to my mother in my white-laced Sunday best and patent-leather Mary Jane shoes as black and as shiny as the hearse sitting outside. There was no Mahalia Jackson singing *Precious Lord, Take My Hand*, no political dignitaries, no famous entertainers—and no Big Ma. She was set against seeing Pop dead so she stayed home, and cousin Bub stayed with her. I don't know if anyone tried to convince her to go, but it would not have made any difference. Even I knew that once Big Ma made up her mind about anything, there would be no unmaking it. I think it gave her permission to pretend Pop was away on a long journey, and that he would come flying through the front door some glad morning. Maybe if I'd known, at six years old, that going to heaven meant he'd never set me in his lap, drive me to school, rock me to sleep, or walk me to Miss Styla's candy store ever again I wouldn't have wanted to go to his funeral either.

Instead, I watched from my hardwood front row seat the parade of people who marched by me to lay eyes on him one last time. Some barely glanced at his lanky, six foot-plus body suited and stretched out like he was sleeping. When the procession finally ended, my mother tucked my hand into hers and walked me to the pine-made casket. The whites of her eyes were stained the same pink color as the carnations in the floral spray perched on a stand nearby. She lifted me up a few inches from the floor and I looked down. I saw that he was wearing a smile, even though he wasn't showing any teeth.

"Bye Pop," I said in a voice just above a hush.

There weren't thousands like the crowd packed into Ebenezer the week before. But it seemed like every black person that lived in Haverstraw was inside the dark paneled, somber sanctuary where Pop served as deacon, and worshipped alongside Big Ma. Everybody—if you were black—knew everybody in Haverstraw. If someone didn't know your name, that someone knew your family. All it took was one question: "Who's your mother?" Or, "What's your daddy's name?"

I grew up a member of this black community made up of long-time residents whose families came to Haverstraw during its heyday as the Brickmaking Capital of the World. Thanks to its rich soil along the Hudson River, the village—thirty miles north of Manhattan—hosted more than forty brickyards in the late nineteenth and early twentieth centuries. But the industry that lured colored men and their families itching to flee the Jim Crow south during that time period dwindled during the Great Depression and died altogether after WWII. Brick was replaced by steel and concrete, and southern-born migrants like Pop had to find other ways to make a living and take care of their families.

I help unpack the minivan and carry my things into my brother's house. The house he owns is the same one my mother bought in 1972 and sold to him after she retired to North Carolina. I place my bags in the bedroom that was once mine, and relax on the twin bed much like the one I had all those years ago. My cell phone rings. The caller ID spells out my husband's three-letter name. He's calling from his part-time job, pretending to be concerned about our travels, relieved that we made it safely. He wants to talk about the state of our marriage. I don't.

He tosses out words like "clarity."

He has clarity.

He's sure of what he wants.

But in the next sentence he isn't sure.

Dangling carrots, dashing hope and broken promises dot the timeline of our last few years together. And now—one pastoral and two marriage counselors later—there's more of the same on the other end of the phone.

A slow burn rises within me.

Exhausted and spent, I feel the sting of tears at the corner of my eyes.

In April 1969, a year after Pop's death, the weather in Haverstraw hung around the mid-fifties. I was sitting on the black grate getting warm when, through his tears, my brother told me "Big Ma's dead."

She died of a broken heart. Everybody said so. After being married to Pop for over forty years, she didn't want to live without him. So she gave up on living for the rest of us.

My sister, brother, and I walked to the George M. Holt Funeral Home the day of her wake. We watched as Mr. Holt finished preparing Big Ma for the viewing. He made a show of putting a pair of cotton gloves on her hands, stiff with death, before resting one on top of the other across her plump waist. She looked like herself but her skin no longer held the fragrance of Pond's Cold Cream or her hair the scent of VO5

Hairdressing. A day later, we were in Fairmount Baptist Church again. This time I sat next to my brother a few rows back from the front where the open casket was placed. This time I cried. This time I understood a new home over in glory meant she wasn't coming back to Haverstraw.

The days seemed quieter after Pop died. But then again Haverstraw was a pretty quiet place. Except when the fire station set off the diaphone foghorn and its deep tones boomed across the village sky to alert the town's people of a fire. The silence grew even louder after Big Ma left to join the great love of her sixty-seven-year life, and took with her the remains of an intact home where a husband and wife loved fiercely and insulated their family with unquestionable protection and security. A sacred space I had no idea I would spend what feels like a lifetime trying to find again.

Slowly, I maneuver the white van along the curved blacktop inside the gates of Mt. Repose in search of Big Ma and Pop. Driving up to the hill to the back of the massive cemetery where the black people are interred, my sister and I spot it at the same time. GUMMER. The name is chiseled in the center of the Grey slab with both names—Henry and Catherine— etched below it. Their April death dates stare back at us. Our three children jump out the car and marvel at the crowded burial ground, unafraid. The young ones venture off, but the two of us stay put. We sit on the sun-warmed grass on opposite sides of the marble stone and lean our heads against it. My sister's eyes fill with tears.

So do mine.

The soft hum that led me to this place grows louder, until the devastating losses of the long ago and the present day converge into one.

Death is imminent. I sense it.

Sitting so near the space that holds two of the earliest loves and losses of my life, I remember its touch. The push and pull between sadness and acceptance as I struggle to hold tight to what's familiar, to what's family, to what's mine.

While seated on the hill at Mt. Repose, an unexpected feeling of comfort begins to settle around me, and I let go and press into the relief of release like I did the moments before I delivered my children into the world. The memories of Pop and Big Ma assisting like midwives, I stop laboring against my fear.

My husband isn't coming back home.

He's in love with someone else.

It's time I give my marriage a final resting place.

I drive the five minutes it takes to get to the lot where we lived with Pop and Big Ma. 143 West Street, the address where I came to live straight from the hospital days after my birth, no longer exists. My haven, the two-story blood-brick house with the slanting side screened-in porch was demolished when developers built the new "Harbors at Haverstraw" waterfront community. The quarter-of-a-million dollar townhomes, condos and luxury apartments is the latest plan to entice city dwellers into moving to the suburb a ferry ride away from Manhattan.

I walk to what would have been our backyard, to the spot where my swing set had been anchored into the ground. I can almost see me as a little girl, four or five years old, singing one of my favorite Sunday School songs—We are Climbing Jacob's Ladder—as I pumped my skinny, ashy legs to make the swing go higher and higher. I bend down to touch a blade of grass and think of Pop and how he would singlehandedly swing his sickle to cut down the tall strands of grass leaning a little too long for us to run through and play games like cigarette tag. I chuckle remembering the childhood favorite, the way my brother and I and our cousins who lived next door would squat down and shout "Winston!" "Salem!" "Pall Mall" just before the unlucky person who wound up being "it" reached out to touch us on our back or shoulder.

I move toward the water. Its tide is yards from the spot of land where our house sat. All the while I hear the echo of Pop's baritone voice, still accented with its southern inflection, warning me, "Don't go down the bank."

Standing on the bank, which isn't much of one anymore, I search for and find a small, flat rock. I toss it into the Hudson with a flip of my wrist and watch it skip across the watery surface until the ripples expand one by one. I pick up another one and try again, and again—like I did when I was young. I look across the river where the new housing development sits. The pristine buildings, predominantly dressed in shades of grey, white and eggshell siding, supplant what came before and is gone forever. Yet they stand as a promise for what comes after.

AN EXPENSIVE LIFE
Linda Fischer

Cossacks swept through a shtetl
and ran down my grandmother's brother,
a boy of fourteen. What I know of him
is nil; he was fourteen and fell
under the horses of soldiers who rode
through the streets creating mayhem—
before the wars, before the Holocaust—
the central fact of his young life
his early death: my grandmother's exodus
out of Vilna the consequence, thus my history.

What it cost her mother to let her go—
a girl of fifteen, alone, to a distant
relation—is all I need to know
of the woman: blood-price paid
for a murdered son. By this act
she chose life for a daughter and withdrew
behind the wall of poverty. Later,
money sent was lost or stolen
as the death machine rolled across Europe.
Then silence—impenetrable, absolute.

I try to imagine her, looking through old
photographs from a dead world, the woman
to whom I owe my existence—family
pictures long gone, her name lost
to memory with the death of my grandmother,
whose naturalization papers—buried in a carton
and forgotten until now—were to finally
unlock the mystery, her mother's name
duly entered on the appropriate line:
Hanna Lintz, the woman whose reach
extends to a fifth generation, her identity
restored and with it a fragment of my past.
What more could she have given?

LEMONS

HOWARD KAPLAN

When he was eighty-five or so and becoming
forgetful—I don't know if this was
just part of getting older or a
little bit of dementia or if the cancer
had come back—his wife
sent him on a walk to the Korean grocer
a few blocks from their house in Whitestone
to pick up a cucumber and two tomatoes
for dinner, and poor papa, he came back
with three lemons.

A NEW LIFE
MARIAN CROTTY

The girl, Hannah, was three and a half weeks old, two months premature, and small for a newborn. It was November but warm out that weekend, and the breeze from the open windows filled the house with the smell of wet soil and dead leaves. Nathan was down the hall, asleep in their bedroom. Rebecca was right there beside her when it happened, nestled under a faded quilt on the guest bed, watching her daughter, willing her to sleep. She turned on the bedside lamp to keep from dozing off in the same bed with Hannah, which the doctor had told her not to do, but then she fell asleep anyway. When she woke a few hours later, gray sunlight filtered through the curtains, and Hannah wasn't breathing.

Rebecca was twenty-five. Since the end of college, she'd worked for an antiques dealer who sold musty wicker furniture out of an old warehouse in Providence. Now she stayed home all day and read self-help books from the library. She'd started with grief but quickly diversified to fashion, home decoration, and easy meals for two. Her favorite books came with photographs of celebrities and clear prohibitions written out in numbered lists. *Low-rise jeans will give pear-shaped women love handles. An entryway, however convenient it may seem to you, is not an appropriate storage space for shoes.* She liked the certainty of right answers and the feeling of building a better life for some future self who might feel like living.

She kept the books hidden in the trunk of her car, away from Nathan who judged people who wanted to be told what to do. He was a safety engineer for a construction company, seven years older, and an atheist, which she was learning was different than a non-religious person who was pretty sure she didn't believe in God. When she cried, he wrapped his arms around her body, but if she tried to talk about Hannah directly, he accused her of smothering him. One night, he said she was like a drowning swimmer, trying to kill him. "And this makes you the lifeguard?"

He kicked off the blankets and fumbled around for the reading glasses he would take with him to the couch.

"I'm trying to picture it," she called after him. "I want to know if you think we're both drowning or if you're just up there watching."

At the support group that met twice a month in the beach-themed living room of a Ronald McDonald House, the other mothers of dead infants reassured her this was typical: women fell apart; men got angry.

"He doesn't yell, though," Rebecca said on the phone to her sister Jenny. "He's crabby and a little bit mean. He wants me to shut up and move on."

"Oh, I doubt it," Jenny said. "I'm sure that's not what's happening. Have you heard of the love languages?"

Jenny was divorced with two kids. She had many theories about relationships, most of which came from The Oprah

Network that she watched on small monitors at the dental office while she cleaned teeth. "I couldn't tell you his love language, but I'd guess it's not words of affirmation. Does he buy you gifts?"

"Windshield wipers, oil changes."

"Well, that would be acts of service."

Jenny thought Nathan should get credit for putting food on the table and for not pressuring her to have sex with him now that she was back on birth control. Her ex-husband had not been so patient. He'd *seemed* patient, but then he'd had an affair. If Rebecca was up to it, she should go ahead and fuck him. Were there blowjobs?

"Jenny."

"I don't like the thought of you losing him. On top of everything else, I don't want to think about you going through this alone."

Rebecca told her sister to mind her own business, but then couldn't stop wondering if Nathan would leave. She didn't think so, but then again, she didn't *not* think so. He worked long hours, stayed up late drinking whiskey and watching *Law and Order*. He did what he could not to be home.

In February, Rebecca initiated sex and then locked herself in the bathroom, crying. Through the filmed windowpane above the bathtub, her neighbors' house lights smeared across the darkness. She sat on the linoleum floor and stared at the linty fur along the heater grate, blowing in small curtains that looked as if they would shake loose but didn't.

In May, Nathan pulled a thick manila envelope from his briefcase and set it on the glass coffee table, frayed on its edges and missing a piece of the outer flap. Divorce papers? She imagined him carrying the envelope around for months, waiting for a respectable amount of time to pass before he was allowed to flee.

"Go ahead," she said. "Tell me."

Nathan was wearing a striped Oxford shirt, still tucked into his dress pants but wrinkled, and his face had the wilted look of the end of a long workweek. "It's a job promotion," he said. "It's a shit ton of money, but it's in Abu Dhabi."

She turned toward him. She had heard of Abu Dhabi but was pretty sure she couldn't find it on a map. "You'd move there?"

"No," he said. "We would. The two of us."

In Abu Dhabi, they lived in a large sandstone villa on a man-made island by the airport with vaulted ceilings and marble floors, and modern furniture rented from a company catalogue. The house was twice the size of their house in Rhode Island, a century newer, filled with chrome appliances and walk-in closets that smelled like cedar, but their subdivision was surrounded by empty lots of gray sand snarled with bulldozers and machines. All night heavy trucks groaned past on the highway and workers hammered through the dark under floodlit cranes. It was July and staggeringly hot. Thick air, no breeze, a bright constant sun angled low in the sky.

Nathan worked six days a week and played soccer in the evenings, coming home at eight o'clock on early nights, nine or ten o'clock if they went out for drinks, but it no longer felt like he was avoiding her so much as learning to be happy. He liked

Abu Dhabi. He saw the money he could earn, the gadgets he could buy, the international community of businessman waiting to befriend him, and Rebecca saw a country of strangers, temporarily living beside each other. Everyone seemed lonely to her and on edge, and whenever she went anywhere by herself, she was aware that people were staring. The Emirati women stared with a kind of recognition, the Emirati men stared with mild curiosity, and the hordes of construction workers, shipped in from India and Pakistan, stared at her with an unblinking intensity that made her look away.

"It's lust," Nathan said. "They think you look like a movie star."

"It's not lust."

She was standing at the shimmering granite countertop, slicing lunch-sized chunks of lasagna into Tupperware containers, and he was moving back and forth behind her, clearing the table.

"Do they bother you?" he said, angry on her behalf. "If they bother you, you can call the police."

"They don't bother me," she said. "They stare. It's tiring."

One day, she took a taxi to a glittering high-ceilinged mall by the marina, where gleaming walkways circled a blue-floored fountain and giant palm trees twinkled with tiny lights. By the front entrance, two men in green construction jumpsuits gaped at a storefront advertisement of a British model in her underwear and then looked at Rebecca as if she were trespassing. She walked past coffee shops of young Emirati men in long white robes, a sea of perfume spritzers, and barely-attended children running in circles. She took an escalator down to a giant fluorescent-lit grocery in the basement and bought a bottle of water and an almond croissant. In the checkout line, a toffee-haired toddler looked up at her from behind his mother's skirts and pointed, his tiny fist squeezing open and closed.

Most days, she stayed home, cooking and cleaning. She watched dubbed American television shows, listened to a British pop radio station, wrote upbeat emails to Jenny and her parents about the lush hotels and skyscrapers, and tried not to think about the loneliness that tugged at her chest like an anchor. Her old life was far away, but her grief felt closer, somehow, and stronger. Alone all day, estranged from everything she knew, her inner life magnified, and all of the thoughts she had tried to bury swam to the surface like a simmering pot of stock dislodging fat from bone. What she didn't want to know came in two lists. The good list—the harder, longer list about Hannah's childhood, the foods she would have liked, the subjects she would have preferred in school, whether her blonde hair and blue eyes would have darkened, and then, the bad list. For instance, was it Rebecca's fault? She dreamed of crushing Hannah's skull in her sleep, suffocating her with blankets, covering her mouth with the palm of her hand.

In the daytime, she drifted in her own private fog, but no one, not even Nathan, seemed to notice. One Saturday in August, they went out with Nathan's coworkers to Trader Vic's, a low-lit French-Polynesian chain restaurant inside a hotel by the beach. A Colombian band was playing salsa on stage, and they sat outside at a table on the grass by the pool where it was quieter—the men, along with one female architect, on one side of the table, and Rebecca on the other side with the wives. The men ordered beer and talked about work; and the women ordered fruity drinks that came with toothpick umbrellas and complimented each other on the cocktail dresses they were all wearing. Rebecca, who had worn linen pants and a loose tunic, explained that before she'd left the United States, she'd purchased clothing to match a diagram she'd found online of "acceptable outfits" for visitors to The Grand Mosque. "I was proud of myself," she said. "I really thought these ugly clothes would help me fit in."

The wives stared at her with a quiet, cliquish disdain, and the female architect, a dark-haired cherub-faced woman from Denmark, gave her a quick smile before abruptly looking away.

"You're overthinking it there," said a short plump blonde whose freckled arms squeezed against the armholes of her dress. "It's not Afghanistan."

A redheaded Australian screwed up her face. "Let them stare at me," she said. "They can get over it. It's not like I'm walking around with my tits out."

She nodded, but it was too late. Rebecca and these women did not belong to the same tribe. Like her, they were housewives with no work visas or job prospects, no real place in this country, but unlike her, this did not depress them.

The next week, Rebecca signed up for an Arabic class that met three times a week in a windowless classroom at a Muslim community center. The teacher, Abdullah, was a disheveled, potbellied man from Jordan who brought a thermos of sticky-sweet tea for them each class and told elaborate jokes about marriage that no one got. "It's funny," he would say. "You must believe me. My bad English ruins the joke."

Often, though, he did make Rebecca laugh simply because he was happy and good-natured and his limited English warped his everyday sentences into strange declarations. One day, when they were learning the names of animals, he hadn't known how to explain the difference between domesticated animals and ones that were wild.

"Pet?" someone had guessed. "Livestock?"

"No!" he said. "The one that eats the peoples."

Nathan didn't understand the practical purpose of learning Arabic in a country where pretty much everyone spoke English, but she could tell he liked the stories she told him about Abdullah and appreciated the effort she was making to like it here. At night, lying beside each other in the pitch dark, the streetlights blocked out by the heavy wall-to-wall drapes, the faint swoosh of traffic in the distance, she pressed her face against the musky crook of his neck, and he listened to her without the usual undercurrent of defensiveness. He laughed at her jokes, heard her complaints, agreed with whatever she told him, though she often had the feeling that he wasn't really listening. Coiled against him, her breathing synced with the rise and fall of his chest, a frightened lonely feeling came over her like a distant warning siren. Did he love her? Had he ever loved her? If he gave himself permission to leave a woman whose child had died, how long would it take him to go?

In October, Nathan had a long weekend for a Muslim holiday Abdullah called "Little Eid," and he surprised her by suggesting a trip to Muscat. They left in a rented car just before sunrise.

Against the early light, the office buildings and construction sites sat dark and idle. Beyond the city, waves of red sand followed the highway for long empty miles.

At the UAE exit checkpoint, the young bearded man behind the Plexiglas looked back and forth between them and their passports for what seemed like a very long time, and asked them a question in English about Nathan's work visa that they couldn't understand. He left the window and an older man replaced him. This man had alert dark eyes, a faint line of hair between his eyebrows, and something kind and curious in his expression that reminded her of Abdullah.

She leaned past Nathan and said hello to him in Arabic and wished him a happy Eid. The questions this time were standard ones—the length of the visit and their final destination—but for some reason, Rebecca found herself saying how surprised she was that her husband was taking a vacation. "He's a stubborn husband," she said. "His love is work. Husbands never love family so much as wives."

She smiled to let the man know that she was making a joke, but he didn't react. She didn't know enough Arabic to explain.

Nathan gave her a quizzical look, and then, miraculously, the guard was laughing. "The wife is in charge," he told Nathan in English, tilting his head toward him and smiling with a kind of happy, reassured exasperation as if to say, *Women, what can you do?*

Past the border, coppery mountains sprang up on either side of the road, and drift sand billowed across the highway. When Rebecca tried the radio, only Islamic chanting and static crackled through the channels. There was a sense of desolation that made her mind wander, and it took a minute to realize that Nathan had asked her a question. "What did you say to him?"

She unfolded the map of Oman they picked up at the border, a thick, detailed map that anticipated lots of English-speaking tourists. Supposedly, their current location was one of the more populated areas, but the landscape looked deserted. "Nothing. I was just talking."

"Tell me."

She opened the glove box and pretended to examine the owner's manual.

"What did you say to him?" he repeated.

"I said you don't like spending time with me."

"No you didn't."

"No," she said. "But it's what I meant to say. My Arabic sucks."

She felt the slow reeling of a fight building. She knew she should apologize but that she wouldn't. Nathan's breathing quickened, settled, then quickened again. "I can't be the only one of us who's ever nice," he said, finally. "I can't always be the one who's trying. Are you listening?"

"Yes," Rebecca said, evenly, though the conversation felt far away. "You are trying, and I am not trying, and this is unfair to you."

They drove southeast through the mountains and into the sun, past date farms, grazing goats, honeycombed limestone forts, and signs warning that rocks might fall. The rocks glinted pink and gold in the sun, and grey-blue shadows floated between the hillsides of shaded homes bordered by irrigation ditches.

She slipped the owner's manual back into the glove box and latched the door.

"I don't know why you haven't left me, but I'm not crazy," she said. "I can tell the difference between you wanting to be with me and you not leaving."

"I love you," he said, calmly. "I want to love you."

"You want to love me?"

They stopped talking. When the hillsides softened, and the narrow roads grew thick with traffic and construction barriers, Nathan stopped for gas and then moved the car to the edge of the parking lot. They leaned against opposite corners of the Toyota's dusty bumper and ate the egg salad sandwiches Rebecca had made.

He pressed his thumbs against the muscles between shoulder and neck, loosening the tension of driving, and she put her hand against his. "Here." She rubbed her fingers against his muscles and tried not to acknowledge the stares of the gas station attendants. "I'm sorry."

She looked at her tennis shoes, a few months old but already discolored by light brown dust, and then Nathan who was squinting at her face, shading his eyes with one hand, balancing the squashed pieces of his sandwich with the other. She couldn't read his expression.

"I'm sorry," she said again. "I'm—"

"I slept with someone."

Rebecca could feel him watching her, but she made herself look forward at the giant wave-shaped awning looming over a sea of gray brick. She half-listened to him telling her that he was sorry, that it was over now, that he hadn't meant to tell her like this. She waited for her anger to kick in, but she felt only a low thrum of queasiness and regret, the murky underwater feeling that something shameful about herself had been revealed.

He wanted to know if they should go home.

"To Abu Dhabi?"

"We can turn around," he said. "We can drive back right now if you want."

"We bought a tent," she said. "We're here."

In Muscat, they parked their car in the old quarter and walked along a sidewalk by the sea, where commercial ships rocked against a stone seawall. Rebecca stared at hillsides of square uniformly white houses and Nathan watched her with the guilty patience of someone who had resigned himself to a long penance. She had thought he meant he'd slept with someone in Rhode Island, but it was the Danish architect whose face she now remembered as patronizing and matronly. She lived in Kuwait, and they had seen each other only a handful of times. Mostly, it had been emails, he said, and mostly, the emails had been about Rebecca. He'd tried to complain about his marriage, but the woman, who had lost her mother in a car accident at age twelve, had always taken Rebecca's side.

"That's supposed to make me feel better?" Rebecca had screamed at him.

The architect had told him to listen without justifying himself or fixing anything, which he seemed to think was a revelation and which Rebecca understood was responsible for his dopey meditative silences, listening as if she were a radio lulling him to sleep.

When it was mid-afternoon, they got back into the car and drove farther south, past rocky cliffs slung over the sea, waves crashing below them, and stopped the car on the edge of a large expanse of empty white sand. They pitched the tent, and walked toward the ocean to watch the sunset. They took off their shoes, walked in the foam of waves, and watched a group of boys in the distance kicking a soccer ball. In comparison to Abu Dhabi's high-rise beach resorts, the beach felt unspoiled but lonesome.

Nathan reached for her hand and a flare of desire lit through her body. How had this happened? He'd taken her across the world to abandon her, and now she wanted him. "I hate you," she'd said again and again in the car, though the more she said it, the more the feeling diminished. She did hate him, a little, but it was a small feeling beside the ache she felt now, in spite of herself, to be loved.

The sun hung above the faint line of the mountains, a pale circle in a dusty pink and yellow sky, and the trees along the shore became dark, prickling shadows. In the distance, the call to prayer sounded, and the boys with the soccer ball paused their game and knelt together on the sand. Rebecca stopped walking and stood still as if she, too, were observing the ritual. She knew she needed to think.

They were putting on their shoes when one of the soccer players called out to them and then came over, holding the hand of a toddler. "Arabie?"

Rebecca nodded and said "little" in Arabic.

The man spoke rapidly, but she understood enough to know he was inviting them to join a celebration. Without asking Nathan, she agreed. They walked through a brick courtyard lined with bougainvillea, and the man explained that because children were permitted to go to both the men's and women's parties, his son would take Rebecca to his wife. It occurred to her that Nathan didn't know any Arabic, but the thought of him silenced and struggling lifted her spirits.

She followed the boy to a large room of low, gold-threaded couches, where dozens of women in ball gowns were eating food and watching a large flat screen television playing music videos in Arabic. Except for the foreign women serving the food, no one's head was covered, and everyone's hair was fixed in elaborate curls and twists. The boy led her to a pretty young woman in a purple rhinestone-studded dress, and Rebecca wondered what kind of person she must look like barging in this way in hiking pants and a long-sleeved t-shirt.

The woman shook her hand and gave her a look of friendly but uncertain welcome. "Thank you," Rebecca said in Arabic. She gestured to the room and said, *"Mash'Allah,"* the word to say in praise of someone while protecting them from jealousy, the verbal equivalent of an evil eye.

Rebecca washed her hands, followed the woman toward a banquet table piled high with lamb and salads, pastries, dates, rice, and then to a circle of young women spread out on the floor. She began to squat down, but the woman pointed to a wooden chair beside a heavy old woman in a wheelchair with a pouch of clear liquid dripping into a vein. She shook the old woman's bony hand and fought the urge to recoil. She thought of how Abdullah had bragged that his country did not have homeless shelters or nursing homes because, in his country, a family did not let you get discarded.

Almost as soon as she sat down, a wave of fatigue washed over her. Nathan—thinking about Nathan—had worn her out. He didn't seem as if he'd wanted to hurt her. In fact, he sounded almost proud of himself. Not proud of the affair but of the way it had changed him. He'd become a better man, a better more empathetic listener, and, preposterously, he wanted Rebecca to tell him he had done a good job.

On the other side of her chair, a group of young women flipped through a photograph album and giggled with nervous excitement. When one of the girls noticed Rebecca watching them, she asked about Rebecca's wedding ring and husband, and Rebecca passed around a picture of Nathan saved on her phone. As she repeated phrases she had practiced many times in her Arabic classes—*We are from America. We live in Abu Dhabi. My husband is Nathan. He works as an engineer*—she knew she was describing a life that no longer belonged to her.

She felt a hand on her shoulder and turned to see the host sitting beside the woman in the wheelchair—her mother? her grandmother—and leaning toward Rebecca. "Engagement book," she said in careful English. "For wedding."

The two women seemed to want to talk about their traditions, and so she asked about their own marriages and if they had engagement pictures.

"Yes," the young woman said tentatively. "Maybe."

Rebecca pointed to the engagement book and then to the old woman. "You have?"

The old woman laughed, shook her head, and then the younger woman explained that there were no cameras to document a wedding so long ago, and Rebecca realized that the old woman had grown up before the oil boom. She had a vague awareness that she should pay attention, that this was a woman who had crossed over from an older, simpler time, but she knew only the words to ask about what she least wanted to know—family.

"Do you have children?"

The woman said yes, eight children. The host was child number seven. Rebecca stared into the woman's face, half expecting her to confess that she had lost other children in childbirth, but she didn't. When the woman asked about Rebecca's family, Rebecca hesitated and then shook her head. It was cruel and complicated to tell the truth, but lying about Hannah made her hate herself.

"Some day," the younger woman said in Arabic. "Insha'Allah."

The women's faces told her that this was sad news, but she couldn't tell if they saw her pain or if this was simply how they would look at any childless woman.

"Haram," said the older woman, squeezing Rebecca's hand. The word made her startle the way it often did, though in this context, she knew it did not mean "forbidden" but something like "what a shame" or "I'm sorry," one of those everyday phrases that sounded poetic but wasn't.

When she saw Nathan across the courtyard, he was in the midst of a dynamic conversation with a young man in glasses, their bodies illuminated by the glow of the lanterns. They were talking fast and laughing, and it took Rebecca a moment to realize that they were speaking English. Of course. The men lived in a wider orbit—were likelier to have been educated abroad, likelier to encounter foreigners at work. Why did Rebecca assume anything else? Men went through life like this—mobile, unselfconscious, unafraid. The world did not expect them to adapt to other people or justify their presence, and this made them strong, but also, stupid. They were not taught to test their visions of themselves against the judgments of strangers, and this meant they could reach adulthood without ever having had to wonder who they were. She had thought that Nathan hid his emotions because he was brave or stingy or else because he simply did not care. It had not occurred to her that he might feel as much as she did but had no tools to navigate the weight of what he felt.

She steadied herself against the house and made her lungs keep breathing. Beyond the latticed stone walls, stars scattered across the black sky, and the ocean crashed against the shore. Nathan lifted his hand to wave and looked at her with an expression of certainty and determination. A man who had been tasked with a great responsibility and believed himself capable of answering. He was ready to stay with her now, ready to make it work. She imagined what advice she would get from Jenny, the support group, the self-help books from the library, but she knew, somehow, that she wouldn't tell anyone. What had happened between them was theirs—a secret thing between them.

On the morning when Hannah had already died but the EMTs had not yet come to look at her body, she had sat on the edge of their king-sized bed with Hannah in her arms, waiting for Nathan to open his eyes. He was lying with a pillow held over his head, restless, trying to fall back asleep. She had woken him up screaming, but then, somehow, his fatigue had won out. Eventually, she would add this moment to the tally of things she held against him, but in the long calm of the gray light, an unseasonably warm November breeze, she had understood. She had wanted him to keep sleeping. She had hoped he would never have to know.

AUTHOR BIOS

STEPHANIE ALLEN'S book, *A Place Between Stations: Stories,* was a finalist for the AWP Award in Short Fiction. Her work has appeared in *Massachusetts Review, Crab Orchard Review* and other publications. She's been awarded a National Endowment for the Arts Literature Fellowship and grants from the Maryland State Arts Council.

ALLISON ALSUP lives in New Orleans. Her work has appeared in the 2014 *O'Henry Prize Stories* and *Best Food Writing* 2015. Her fiction has won story contests from *A Room of Her Own Foundation, New Millennium Writings,* and *Philadelphia Stories.* She is currently working on a novel.

GAYLORD BREWER is a professor at Middle Tennessee State University, where he founded and for more than 20 years edited the journal *Poems & Plays.* His most recent books are a ninth collection of poetry, *Country of Ghost Red Hen,* and the cookbook-memoir *The Poet's Guide to Food, Drink, & Desire* from Stephen F. Austin, both in 2015.

BILL BROWN is the author of nine poetry collections. His newest, *Elemental,* from A Taos Press, has been nominated for The Weatherford Award and the Southern Independent

Booksellers Award. His recent work has appeared in *Tar River Poetry, River Styx, Cloud Bank, Birmingham Poetry Review, Big Muddy,* and *POEM.*

MARIAN CROTTY is an assistant professor of writing at Loyola University Maryland, and an assistant editor at *The Common.* Her writing has appeared in literary journals such as *The Gettysburg Review, The Southern Review,* and *The New England Review.* She currently is working on a novel.

MICHAEL ESTES teaches at Jefferson Community and Technical College in Louisville, KY. His poems have appeared in *Boulevard, Catch Up, Court Green, Fourteen Hills,* and elsewhere.

LINDA FISCHER, a two-time Pushcart Prize nominee, was a merit award winner in *Atlanta Review's* Poetry 2013 International Competition and a finalist in 2014. Her poems are published or forthcoming in *Valparaiso Poetry Review, Josephine Quarterly, Iodine Poetry Journal, Ibbetson Street, Muddy River Poetry Review, Poetry Porch, Schuylkill Valley Journal,* and elsewhere. She has two chapbooks, *Raccoon Afternoons* and *Glory* from Finishing Line Press.

BRANDON FRENCH is the only daughter of an opera singer and a Spanish dancer, born in Chicago at the end of the Second World War. She has been assistant editor of *Modern Teen Magazine,* a topless Pink Pussycat cocktail waitress, an assistant professor of English at Yale, a published film scholar, a playwright and screenwriter, director of development at Columbia Pictures Television, an award-winning advertising copywriter and creative director, a psychoanalyst in private practice, and a mother. Twenty-five of her stories have been accepted for publication by literary journals, she was nominated twice for the Kirkwood Prize in Fiction at UCLA, and she was an award winner in the 2015 Chicago Tribune Nelson Algren Short Story Contest.

KIM GARCIA is the author of *The Brighter House*, winner of the 2015 White Pine Press Poetry Prize, and *Drone*, winner of the 2015 Backwaters Prize, and *Madonna Magdalene*, released by Turning Point Books in 2006. Her chapbook *Tales of the Sisters* won the 2015 *Sow's Ear Poetry Review* Chapbook Contest. Her poems have appeared in such journals as *Crab Orchard Review, Crazyhorse, Mississippi Review, Nimrod* and *Subtropics*. Her work has been featured on *The Writer's Almanac*. Recipient of the 2014 Lynda Hull Memorial Prize, an AWP Intro Writing Award, a Hambidge Fellowship and an Oregon Individual Artist Grant, Garcia teaches creative writing at Boston College.

CONNIE GREEN lives in Tennessee and writes a newspaper column, poetry, and young people's novels, *The War at Home* and *Emmy*. She has two chapbooks, *Slow Children Playing* and *Regret Comes to Tea*, from Finishing Line Press; her collection, *Household Inventory*, won the 2013 Brick Road Poetry Award and is available from Brick Road Press.

JANET HAGELGANS holds a degree in Criminal Justice from the University of Maryland. Her poetry has appeared in the *Thrush Poetry Journal*, *Atticus Review*, *Potomac Review*, and *Common Ground Review*, and is forthcoming in the *Cider Press Review*.

KYLE HAYS currently lives in Stillwater, OK, where he is pursuing an MFA in Fiction. His fiction has recently appeared in *The Seattle Review*.

JULIA JOHNSON received an MFA in creative writing from American University. Her poems have appeared in *Southern Poetry Review*, *Poet Lore*, *Timber Creek Review*, and *Tundra*, among others. Her chapbook, *The Tea of the Unforeseen Berry*, was published by Finishing Line Press. She is a Fellow of the Virginia Center for the Creative Arts.

WILLIAM JOLLIFF is a native of Magnetic Springs, Ohio, and currently serves as a professor of English at George Fox University. He is also a contributor and editor for the journal *Windhover* and his poems, articles, and review have appeared in *West Branch*, *Southern Humanities Review*, *Southern Poetry Review*, *Appalachian Journal*, *Poet Lore*, and *Midwest Quarterly*. His new collection, *Twisted Shapes of Light*, was published last May in the Poiema Poetry Series from *Cascade Press*.

HOWARD KAPLAN lives in Washington DC. He is a recipient of fellowships and residencies from the MacDowell Colony, Bread Loaf Writer's Conference, and the Edward Albee Foundation.

EMILY KOON is a fiction writer from North Carolina. She has work in *Midway Journal, Portland Review, Atticus Review,* and other places and is the winner of *The Conium Review* 2015 Innovative Fiction Contest.

HARRIS LAHTI's work has appeared in *Bull: Men's Fiction* and *LowCard Magazine.* He lives in Warwick, New York.

JEANNE LARSEN has published two books of poetry, *Why We Make Gardens [& other Poems],* and *James Cook in Search of Terra Incognita,* as well as two of literary translations from Chinese, and four novels. She teaches in the Jackson Center for Creative Writing at Hollins University in Roanoke, Virginia.

PETER MAKUCK is a twice winner of the annual Brockman-Campbell Award for best book of poetry published by a North Carolinian in 1988 and 2011. He has authored five volumes of poetry; the last is *Long Lens: New & Selected Poems* (BOA Editions, Ltd., 2010). Forthcoming in September 2016 from the same publisher is *Mandatory Evacuation.* In 2013, Syracuse University Press published his third collection of short stories, *Allegiance and Betrayal.* His essays, reviews, poems, and stories have appeared in *The Hudson Review, North American Review, Southern Poetry Review,* and *The Sewanee Review.* Founder and editor of *Tar River Poetry* from 1978 to 2006, Peter Makuck is a Distinguished Professor Emeritus at East Carolina University.

MATT MORGAN, a native Mississippian, currently lives in Michigan, where he is in the MFA program at Western Michigan University. His work has appeared in *The Milo Review* and *The Monarch Review*.

KATRINA NORFLEET is a communications writer/editor with a background in public health and medical science writing. Her creative nonfiction work appears in *Penn-Union* and in several anthologies, including *Wisdom Has a Voice: Every Daughter's Memory of Mother*. She lives in Maryland, and is mother to an adult son and daughter.

KEN POYNER'S work has lately been seen in *Analog, Café Irreal, The Journal of Microliterature, Blue Collar Review*, and many wonderful places. His latest book of bizarre short fiction, *Constant Animals,* is available online.

RYAN RIDGE is the author of the story collection *Hunters & Gamblers,* the poetry collection *Ox,* as well as the novella, *American Homes.* His new collection, *Camouflage Country,* co-written with Mel Bosworth, is out now from Queen's Ferry Press. His previous work can be found in *NERVE, Fanzine, FLAUNT Magazine, The Los Angeles Review, The Santa Monica Review, Salt Hill, DIAGRAM,* and *Sleepingfish.* He is currently a visiting professor of creative writing at the University of Louisville.

PENELOPE SCAMBLY SCHOTT is the author of a novel, ten full-length poetry books, and six chapbooks. Her verse biography, *A is for Anne: Mistress Hutchinson Disturbs the Commonwealth*, won an Oregon Book Award for Poetry. Recent books include *Lovesong for Dufur* and *Lillie Was a Goddess, Lillie Was a Whore*. *How I Became an Historian* was published in 2014. She lives in Portland and Dufur, Oregon where she teaches a poetry workshop.

DAVID WHITE'S poetry has appeared in or is upcoming in *THRUSH Poetry Journal, Salamander, Paper Nautilus, PRISM international, Southwestern American Literature,* and elsewhere. He currently teaches creative writing in Tempe, Arizona.

RUTH WILLIAMS is the author of *Conveyance* (Dancing Girl Press, 2012). Her poetry has appeared in *Michigan Quarterly Review, jubilat, Sou'wester, Fourteen Hills,* and *Third Coast,* among others. Currently, she is an Assistant Professor of English at William Jewell College.

CPSIA information can be obtained
at www.ICGtesting.com
Printed in the USA
FFOW05n0211010316

9 780988 949355